SPECIES

I0520443

EDITED BY THURSTON HOWL

A THURSTON HOWL PUBLICATIONS BOOK

ISBN 978-1-945247-22-4

SPECIES: WOLVES

A Thurston Howl Publications Book
Published by Thurston Howl Publications
thurstonhowlpublications.com
Lansing, MI

jonathan.thurstonhowlpub@gmail.com

Cover design by Thurston Howl
Cover art by Daniie © 2017
Profile illustrations by Daniie © 2017

Printed in the United States of America
10 9 8 7 6 5 4 3 2 1

Contents

INTRODUCTION
Thurston Howl

Thurston Howl is the editor-in-chief of Thurston Howl Publications. His short stories have appeared in HEAT, Typewriter Emergencies, ROAR, Wolf Warriors, Civilized Beasts, *and* Purrfect Tails. *His essay collection* Furries Among Us *won an Ursa Major Award in 2016, and his story "Concerto" won a Creative Expression Award in the college magazine* COLLAGE. *When he is not writing, editing, or reading, he is curled up with his dog (who thinks she is a cat) Temerita and his boyfriend Tabsley (who occasionally mistakes the book collection for bamboo and tries either climbing or eating it).*

Having edited three successful volumes of *Wolf Warriors,* a charity anthology series for the National Wolfwatcher Coalition, I can say that I have seen wolves in hundreds of perspectives. Symbolically, historically, and culturally, wolves are a diverse image. In the corpus of anthropomorphic animal literature, wolves are just as multi-faceted, ranging from a violent trickster to a pack leader.

So, it is with great honor that I bring to you the first volume of the SPECIES anthology series, Wolves. As will be the tradition of the series, it will start with some of the more classic stories of anthropomorphic animals, possibly show some furry stories from the past couple of decades, and original work, too!

This variety will include the many faces of the anthropomorphic wolf in literature: alpha wolves, tricksters, pack animals, howling wolves, werewolves, and even our monstrous wolves. As the point of this series is to showcase some of the best species-specific stories, I hope that when you go back to shelve this book in your personal library you feel just a little bit wolfier.

Ever onward, dear reader.

Thurston Howl

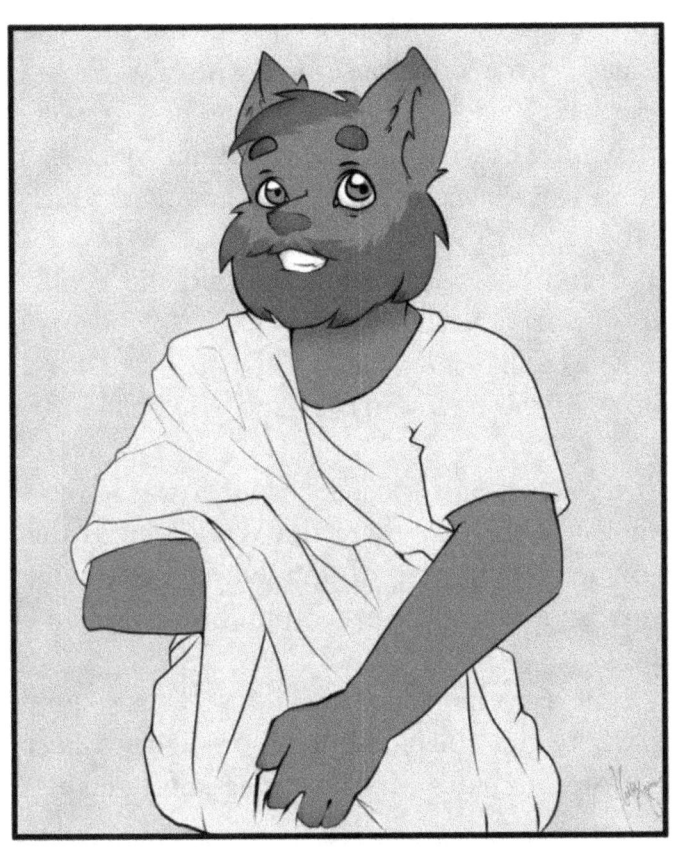

THE DOG AND THE WOLF
Aesop; trans. George Flyer Townsend

Aesop, who is supposed to have lived around 600 BCE, is best known for his collection of Fables. Little is known about his actual life other than his slavery and his writings. However, his legacy is long-lasting through his moralistic tales, many of which featured the wolf as a trickster characterized by greed and hunger.

A gaunt Wolf was almost dead with hunger when he happened to meet a House-dog who was passing by. "Ah, Cousin," said the Dog. "I knew how it would be; your irregular life will soon be the ruin of you. Why do you not work steadily as I do, and get your food regularly given to you?"

"I would have no objection," said the Wolf, "if I could only get a place."

"I will easily arrange that for you," said the Dog; "come with me to my master and you shall share my work."

So the Wolf and the Dog went towards the town together. On the way there the Wolf noticed that the hair on a certain part of the Dog's neck was very much worn away, so he asked him how that had come about.

"Oh, it is nothing," said the Dog. "That is only the place where the collar is put on at night to keep me chained up; it chafes a bit, but one soon gets used to it."

"Is that all?" said the Wolf. "Then good-bye to you, Master Dog."

Better starve free than be a fat slave.

YSENGRIMUS
Anonymous; trans. Rayah James

Rayah is a bunny with a Bachelor of Arts in English from Middle Tennessee State University. During her college career, she worked on school newspapers and as a writing consultant. When Rayah is not immersed in a story that she's reading or writing, she can be found perusing bookstores and thrift stores, hanging out with some of her best wolf friends, or on a Netflix binge with a cat or dog by her side.

Isengrim found himself wandering into a dew-covered field in the early morning light. He usually preferred to stay in the woods, but today he had to scavenge for food. There were hungry pups to feed at home he was responsible for. As he reached the edge of the clearing, he noticed a flash of red in his peripheral. That stealthy fox, Renard, must have beaten him here again. Insengrim's stomach growled; Renard looked particularly tasty, he noticed. Wolves didn't always catch foxes, but it wasn't out of the question. Isengrim seized the opportunity to sneak up on the smaller canid. It wasn't until it was too late to run that Renard looked up from his watch on a flock of small birds and noticed the much larger Isengrim hovering over him.

"I hope the prey you are looking for comes to you today, my canine brother," Renard blurted out, stuttering to the wolf. "I pray you have a g-good hunt."

"Oh, I think I have…" said Isengrim with a low growl. "I think your wish has come true."

Renard cowered as Isengrim licked his chops.

"I think you are the answer to your own prayers Renard. I found *you*. I couldn't imagine better or easier prey."

Renard sought escape, but was met by Insegrim's large paw in his path and a warning growl.

"Oh no, you're not going anywhere. The only place you are going is between my jaws, and I hope you will come willingly."

The fox whimpered.

"Don't complain, little fox. The way I see it, this has a lot of benefits for both of us. Chiefly, I will be fed, and I am so desperately in need. And you…Well, you won't have to hunt for food anymore. No, you will be warm in my stomach and safe from all other predators that might want to eat you. I'll protect you like a suit of armor, and I will carry you so you won't become tired. Other larger predators surely won't be as reasonable as I either. Come now, see what I am offering you and be reasonable. I've offered to be your horse and you to be my rider. I'm not ashamed to serve you, my dear fox. I wish I were able to serve more of canid-kind. It's true that I haven't always got along with everyone from our kind...especially the smaller types like yourself, but I haven't been a fool or resorted to violence. I'm not that type, you see. No, I don't like to make my enemy afraid with violent outbursts. It's too messy. No, I prefer to be patient. I find that if a person let's hatred get the best of him, then he will get his vengeance quicker. That aside though, you and I have both wished for you to appear in my path today, didn't we? And how wonderful it is that this wish has come true? Now, like I said, your kind and mine are family, but we haven't always gotten along. Even you have been a disappointment to me. You have stolen my prey in these fields, the food that I was going to take back to my wife and my children. I'm a good sport though, and I have prepared a nice warm place in my stomach just for you. All you have to do is come in." The wolf opened his jaws.

"I'd be happy to have you come in now," he urged Renard, grazing his teeth gingerly now across the small fox's back.

It was in his instinct to run, but Renard stayed still instead as Isengrim began to taunt him further by pulling hair out on both sides of his body. The fox was like a mouse taunted and finally captured and turned on his back to be played with before eaten. Just like the mouse gives up at that point, out of fear, so had Renard. He regretted staying put, but he feared running more. He chose to sit and endure. *If he only turned his head*, Renard thought. *Then I could run away. If I could run away, then I wouldn't come back to this field for all the prey in the world.* He knew this would not end well.

The massive wolf had finally encircled his cunning enemy. He was confident now, perhaps overly so. Renard was finally well and truly in his grasp. He didn't want to choke the fox by fear to begin with though. No, he wanted the fear to do the work first. He wanted the vulpine to feel how powerless he'd become in this situation, but he could only wait so long. The wolf's teeth sank into the fox's neck once, twice, and now a third time. His teeth rang like a bell or an anvil as they clamped down on his prey. The fox yelped in pain.

"Don't be scared," Isengrim cooed. "I haven't even really started yet. These old teeth shouldn't be hurting you so much. Why are you hesitating? You know that this door into my warm abode won't always stay open. They are open now though, and I have invited you in. Why are you making this so difficult? Why are you just cowering there? You have to come quickly. If you are wise, you will take my offer and receive all the benefits I have offered you before someone else does."

THE WHITE WOLF
Andrew Lang

Andrew Lang, born in 1844, is best known for his collection of fairy tales and folktales. He was educated at the Edinburgh Academy and created the collections known as the Fairy Books. He published many wolf stories throughout his career before dying in 1912.

Once upon a time there was a king who had three daughters; they were all beautiful, but the youngest was the fairest of the three. Now it happened that one day their father had to set out for a tour in a distant part of his kingdom. Before he left, his youngest daughter made him promise to bring her back a wreath of wild flowers. When the king was ready to return to his palace, he bethought himself that he would like to take home presents to each of his three daughters; so he went into a jeweler's shop and bought a beautiful necklace for the eldest princess; then he went to a rich merchant's and bought a dress embroidered in gold and silver thread for the second princess, but in none of the flower shops nor in the market could he find the wreath of wild flowers that his youngest daughter had set her heart on. So he had to set out on his homeward way without it. Now his journey led him through a thick forest. While he was still about four miles distant from his palace, he noticed a white wolf squatting on the roadside, and, behold! on the head of the wolf, there was a wreath of wild flowers.

Then the king called to the coachman, and ordered him to get down from his seat and fetch him the wreath from the wolf's head. But the wolf heard the order and said: "My lord and king, I will let you have the wreath, but I must have something in return."

"What do you want?" answered the king. "I will gladly give you rich treasure in exchange for it."

"I do not want rich treasure," replied the wolf. "Only promise to give me the first thing that meets you on your way to your castle. In three days I shall come and fetch it."

And the king thought to himself: "I am still a good long way from home, I am sure to meet a wild animal or a bird on the road, it will be quite safe to promise." So he consented, and carried the wreath away with him. But all along the road he met no living creature till he turned into the palace gates, where his youngest daughter was waiting to welcome him home.

That evening the king was very sad, remembering his promise; and when he told the queen what had happened, she too shed bitter tears. And the youngest princess asked them why they both looked so sad, and why they wept. Then her father told her what a price he would have to pay for the wreath of wild flowers he had brought borne to her, for in three days a white wolf would come and claim her and carry her away, and they would never see her again. But the queen thought and thought, and at last she hit upon a plan.

There was in the palace a servant maid the same age and the same height as the princess, and the queen dressed her up in a beautiful dress belonging to her daughter, and determined to give her to the white wolf, who would never know the difference.

On the third day the wolf strode into the palace yard and up the great stairs, to the room where the king and queen were seated.

"I have come to claim your promise," he said. "Give me your youngest daughter."

Then they led the servant maid up to him, and he said to her: "You must mount on my back, and I will take you to my castle." And with these words he swung her on to his back and left the palace.

When they reached the place where he had met the king and given him the wreath of wild flowers, he stopped, and told her to dismount that they might rest a little.

So they sat down by the roadside.

"I wonder," said the wolf, "what your father would do if this forest belonged to him?"

And the girl answered: "My father is a poor man, so he would cut down the trees, and saw them into planks, and he would sell the planks, and we should never be poor again; but would always have enough to eat."

Then the wolf knew that he had not got the real princess, and he swung the servant-maid on to his back and carried her to the castle. And he strode angrily into the king's chamber, and spoke.

"Give me the real princess at once. If you deceive me again I will cause such a storm to burst over your palace that the walls will fall in, and you will all be buried in the ruins."

Then the king and the queen wept, but they saw there was no escape. So they sent for their youngest daughter, and the king said to her: "Dearest child, you must go with the white wolf, for I promised you to him, and I must keep my word."

So the princess got ready to leave her home; but first she went to her room to fetch her wreath of wild flowers, which she took with her. Then the white wolf swung her on his back and bore her away. But when they came to the place where he had rested with the servant-maid, he told her to dismount that they might rest for a little at the roadside. Then he turned to her and said: "I wonder what your father would do if this forest belonged to him?"

And the princess answered: "My father would cut down the trees and turn it into a beautiful park and gardens, and he and his courtiers would come and wander among the glades in the summer time."

"This is the real princess," said the wolf to himself.

But aloud he said: "Mount once more on my back, and I will bear you to my castle."

And when she was seated on his back he set out through the woods, and he ran, and ran, and ran, till at last he stopped in front of a stately courtyard, with massive gates.

"This is a beautiful castle," said the princess, as the gates swung back and she stepped inside. "If only I were not so far away from my father and my mother!"

But the wolf answered: "At the end of a year we will pay a visit to your father and mother."

And at these words the white furry skin slipped from his back, and the princess saw that he was not a wolf at all, but a beautiful youth, tall and stately; and he gave her his hand, and led her up the castle stairs.

One day, at the end of half a year, he came into her room and said: "My dear one, you must get ready for a wedding. Your eldest sister is going to be married, and I will take you to your father's palace. When the wedding is over, I shall come and fetch you home. I will whistle outside the gate, and when you hear me, pay no heed to what your father or mother say, leave your dancing and feasting, and come to me at once; for if I have to leave without you, you will never find your way back alone through the forests."

When the princess was ready to start, she found that he had put on his white fur skin, and was changed back into the wolf; and he swung her on to his back, and set out with her to her father's palace, where he left her, while he himself returned home alone. But, in the evening, he went back to fetch her, and, standing outside the palace gate, he gave a long, loud whistle. In the midst of her dancing the princess heard the sound, and at once she went to him, and he swung her on his back and bore her away to his castle.

Again, at the end of half a year, the prince came into her room, as the white wolf, and said: "Dear heart, you must prepare for the wedding of your second sister. I will take you to your father's palace to-day, and we will remain there together till to-morrow morning."

So they went together to the wedding. In the evening, when the two were alone together, he dropped his fur skin, and, ceasing to be a wolf, became a prince again. Now they did not know that the princess's mother was hidden in the room. When she saw the white skin lying on the floor, she crept out of the room, and sent a servant to fetch the skin and to burn it in the kitchen fire. The moment the flames touched the skin there was a fearful clap of thunder heard, and the prince disappeared out of the palace gate in a whirlwind, and returned to his palace alone.

But the princess was heart-broken, and spent the night weeping bitterly. Next morning she set out to find her way back to the castle, but she wandered through the woods and forests, and she could find no path or track to guide her. For fourteen days she roamed in the forest, sleeping under the trees, and living upon wild berries and roots, and at last she reached a little house. She opened the door and went in, and found the wind seated in the room all by himself, and she spoke to the wind and said:

"Wind, have you seen the white wolf?"

And the wind answered: "All day and all night I have been blowing round the world, and I have only just come home; but I have not seen him."

But he gave her a pair of shoes, in which, he told her, she would be able to walk a hundred miles with every step. Then she walked through the air till she reached a star, and she said: "Tell me, star, have you seen the white wolf?"

And the star answered: "I have been shining all night, and I have not seen him."

But the star gave her a pair of shoes, and told her that if she put them on she would be able to walk two hundred miles at a stride. So she drew them on, and she walked to the moon, and she said: "Dear moon, have you not seen the white wolf?"

But the moon answered, "All night long I have been sailing through the heavens, and I have only just come home; but I did not see him."

But he gave her a pair of shoes, in which she would be able to cover four hundred miles with every stride. So she went to the sun, and said: "Dear sun, have you seen the white wolf?"

And the sun answered, "Yes, I have seen him, and he has chosen another bride, for he thought you had left him, and would never return, and he is preparing for the wedding. But I will help you. Here are a pair of shoes. If you put these on you will be able to walk on glass or ice, and to climb the steepest places. And here is a spinning-wheel, with which you will be able to spin moss into silk. When you leave me you will reach a glass mountain. Put on the shoes that I have given you and with them you will be able to climb it quite easily. At the summit you will find the palace of the white wolf."

Then the princess set out, and before long she reached the glass mountain, and at the summit she found the white wolf's palace, as the sun had said.

But no one recognized her, as she had disguised herself as an old woman, and had wound a shawl round her head. Great preparations were going on in the palace for the wedding, which was to take place next day. Then the princess, still disguised as an old woman, took out her spinning-wheel, and began to spin moss into silk. And as she spun the new bride passed by, and seeing the moss turn into silk, she said to the old woman: "Little mother, I wish you would give me that spinning-wheel."

And the princess answered, "I will give it to you if you will allow me to sleep to-night on the mat outside the prince's door."

And the bride replied, "Yes, you may sleep on the mat outside the door."

So the princess gave her the spinning-wheel. And that night, winding the shawl all round her, so that no one could recognize her, she lay down on the mat outside the white wolf's door. And when everyone in the palace was asleep she began to tell the whole of her story. She told how she had been one of three sisters, and that she had been the youngest and the fairest of the three, and that her father had betrothed her to a white wolf. And she told how she had gone first to the wedding of one sister, and then with her husband to the wedding of the other sister, and how her mother had ordered the servant to throw the white fur skin into the kitchen fire. And then she told of her wanderings through the forest; and of how she had sought the white wolf weeping; and how the wind and star and moon and sun had befriended her, and had helped her to reach his palace. And when the white wolf heard all the story, he knew that it was his first wife, who had sought him, and had found him, after such great dangers and difficulties.

But he said nothing, for he waited till the next day, when many guests—kings and princes from far countries—were coming to his wedding. Then, when all the guests were assembled in the banqueting hall, he spoke to them and said: "Hearken to me, ye kings and princes, for I have something to tell you. I had lost the key of my treasure casket, so I ordered a new one to be made; but I have since found the old one. Now, which of these keys is the better?"

Then all the kings and royal guests answered:

"Certainly the old key is better than the new one."

"Then," said the wolf, "if that is so, my former bride is better than my new one."

And he sent for the new bride, and he gave her in marriage to one of the princes who was present, and then he turned to his guests, and said: "And here is my former bride"—and the beautiful princess was led into the room and seated beside him on his throne. "I thought she had forgotten me, and that she would never return. But she has sought me everywhere, and now we are together once more we shall never part again."

THE GRAY WOLF
George MacDonald

George MacDonald, born 1824, was one of the founding fathers of the fantasy genre. He was also a mentor to Lewis Carroll. Some of his major works include Lilith, Phantastes, *and* The Princess and the Goblin. *However, he was also a fan of werewolf literature in the nineteenth century. The following piece is his contribution to contemporary werewolf literature.*

One evening-twilight in spring, a young English student, who had wandered northwards as far as the outlying fragments of Scotland called the Orkney and Shetland Islands, found himself on a small island of the latter group, caught in a storm of wind and hail, which had come on suddenly. It was in vain to look about for any shelter; for not only did the storm entirely obscure the landscape, but there was nothing around him save a desert moss.

At length, however, as he walked on for mere walking's sake, he found himself on the verge of a cliff, and saw, over the brow of it, a few feet below him, a ledge of rock, where he might find some shelter from the blast, which blew from behind. Letting himself down by his hands, he alighted upon something that crunched beneath his tread, and found the bones of many small animals scattered about in front of a little cave in the rock, offering the refuge he sought. He went in, and sat upon a stone. The storm increased in violence, and as the darkness grew he became uneasy, for he did not relish the thought of spending the night in the cave. He had parted from his companions on the opposite side of the island, and it added to his uneasiness that they must be full of apprehension about him. At last there came a lull in the storm, and the same instant he heard a footfall, stealthy and light as that of a wild beast, upon the bones at the mouth of the cave. He started up in some fear, though the least thought might have satisfied him that there could be no very dangerous animals upon the island. Before he had time to think, however, the face of a woman appeared in the opening. Eagerly the wanderer spoke. She started at the sound of his voice. He could not see her well, because she was turned towards the darkness of the cave.

"Will you tell me how to find my way across the moor to Shielness?" he asked.

"You cannot find it to-night," she answered, in a sweet tone, and with a smile that bewitched him, revealing the whitest of teeth.

"What am I to do, then?"

"My mother will give you shelter, but that is all she has to offer."

"And that is far more than I expected a minute ago," he replied. "I shall be most grateful."

She turned in silence and left the cave. The youth followed. She was barefooted, and her pretty brown feet went catlike over the sharp stones, as she led the way down a rocky path to the shore. Her garments were scanty and torn, and her hair blew tangled in the wind. She seemed about five and twenty, lithe and small. Her long fingers kept clutching and pulling nervously at her skirts as she went. Her face was very gray in complexion, and very worn, but delicately formed, and smooth-skinned. Her thin nostrils were tremulous as eyelids, and her lips, whose curves were faultless, had no color to give sign of indwelling blood. What her eyes were like he could not see, for she had never lifted the delicate films of her eyelids.

At the foot of the cliff. they came upon a little hut leaning against it, and having for its inner apartment a natural hollow within. Smoke was spreading over the face of the rock, and the grateful odour of food gave hope to the hungry student. His guide opened the door of the cottage; he followed her in, and saw a woman bending over a fire in the middle of the floor. On the fire lay a large fish broiling. The daughter spoke a few words, and the mother turned and welcomed the stranger. She had an old and very wrinkled, but honest face, and looked troubled. She dusted the only chair in the cottage, and placed it for him by the side of the fire, opposite the one window, whence he saw a little patch of yellow sand over which the spent waves spread themselves out listlessly. Under this window there was a bench, upon which the daughter threw herself in an unusual posture, resting her chin upon her hand. A moment after, the youth caught the first glimpse of her blue eyes. They were fixed upon him with a strange look of greed, amounting to craving, but, as if aware that they belied or betrayed her, she dropped them instantly. The moment she veiled them, her face, notwithstanding its colorless complexion, was almost beautiful.

When the fish was ready, the old woman wiped the deal table, steadied it upon the uneven floor, and covered it with a piece of fine table-linen. She then laid the fish on a wooden platter, and invited the guest to help himself. Seeing no other provision, he pulled from his pocket a hunting knife, and divided a portion from the fish, offering it to the mother first.

"Come, my lamb," said the old woman; and the daughter approached the table. But her nostrils and mouth quivered with disgust.

The next moment she turned and hurried from the hut.

"She doesn't like fish," said the old woman, "and I haven't anything else to give her."

"She does not seem in good health," he rejoined.

The woman answered only with a sigh, and they ate their fish with the help of a little rye bread. As they finished their supper, the youth heard the sound as of the pattering of a dog's feet upon the sand close to the door; but ere he had time to look out of the window, the door opened, and the young woman entered. She looked better, perhaps from having just washed her face. She drew a stool to the corner of the fire opposite him. But as she sat down, to his bewilderment, and even horror, the student spied a single drop of blood on her white skin within her torn dress. The woman brought out a jar of whisky, put a rusty old kettle on the fire, and took her place in front of it. As soon as the water boiled, she proceeded to make some toddy in a wooden bowl.

Meantime the youth could not take his eyes off the young woman, so that at length he found himself fascinated, or rather bewitched. She kept her eyes for the most part veiled with the loveliest eyelids fringed with darkest lashes, and he gazed entranced; for the red glow of the little oil-lamp covered all the strangeness of her complexion. But as soon as he met a stolen glance out of those eyes unveiled, his soul shuddered within him. Lovely face and craving eyes alternated fascination and repulsion.

The mother placed the bowl in his hands. He drank sparingly, and passed it to the girl. She lifted it to her lips, and as she tasted—only tasted it—looked at him. He thought the drink must have been drugged and have affected his brain. Her hair smoothed itself back, and drew her forehead backwards with it; while the lower part of her face projected towards the bowl, revealing, ere she sipped, her dazzling teeth in strange prominence. But the same moment the vision vanished; she returned the vessel to her mother, and rising, hurried out of the cottage.

Then the old woman pointed to a bed of heather in one corner with a murmured apology; and the student, wearied both with the fatigues of the day and the strangeness of the night, threw himself upon it, wrapped in his cloak. The moment he lay down, the storm began afresh, and the wind blew so keenly through the crannies of the hut, that it was only by drawing his cloak over his head that he could protect himself from its currents. Unable to sleep, he lay listening to the uproar which grew in violence, till the spray was dashing against the window. At length the door opened, and the young woman came in, made up the fire, drew the bench before it, and lay down in the same strange posture, with her chin propped on her hand and elbow, and her face turned towards the youth. He moved a little; she dropped her head, and lay on her face, with her arms crossed beneath her forehead. The mother had disappeared.

Drowsiness crept over him. A movement of the bench roused him, and he fancied he saw some four-footed creature as tall as a large dog trot quietly out of the door. He was sure he felt a rush of cold wind. Gazing fixedly through the darkness, he thought he saw the eyes of the damsel encountering his, but a glow from the falling together of the remnants of the fire revealed clearly enough that the bench was vacant. Wondering what could have made her go out in such a storm, he fell fast asleep.

In the middle of the night he felt a pain in his shoulder, came broad awake, and saw the gleaming eyes and grinning teeth of some animal close to his face. Its claws were in his shoulder, and its mouth in the act of seeking his throat. Before it had fixed its fangs, however, he had its throat in one hand, and sought his knife with the other. A terrible struggle followed; but regardless of the tearing claws, he found and opened his knife. He had made one futile stab, and was drawing it for a surer, when, with a spring of the whole body, and one wildly contorted effort, the creature twisted its neck from his hold, and with something betwixt a scream and a howl, darted from him. Again he heard the door open; again the wind blew in upon him, and it continued blowing; a sheet of spray dashed across the floor, and over his face. He sprung from his couch and bounded to the door.

It was a wild night-dark, but for the flash of whiteness from the waves as they broke within a few yards of the cottage; the wind was raving, and the rain pouring down the air. A gruesome sound as of mingled weeping and howling came from somewhere in the dark. He turned again into the hut and closed the door, but could find no way of securing it.

The lamp was nearly out, and he could not be certain whether the form of the young woman was upon the bench or not. Overcoming a strong repugnance, he approached it, and put out his hands—there was nothing there. He sat down and waited for the daylight: he dared not sleep any more.

When the day dawned at length, he went out yet again, and looked around. The morning was dim and gusty and gray. The wind had fallen, but the waves were tossing wildly. He wandered up and down the little strand, longing for more light.

At length he heard a movement in the cottage. By and by the voice of the old woman called to him from the door.

"You're up early, sir. I doubt you didn't sleep well."

"Not very well," he answered. "But where is your daughter?"

"She's not awake yet," said the mother. "I'm afraid I have but a poor breakfast for you. But you'll take a dram and a bit of fish. It's all I've got."

Unwilling to hurt her, though hardly in good appetite, he sat down at the table. While they were eating, the daughter came in, but turned her face away and went to the farther end of the hut. When she came forward after a minute or two, the youth saw that her hair was drenched, and her face whiter than before. She looked ill and faint, and when she raised her eyes, all their fierceness had vanished, and sadness had taken its place. Her neck was now covered with a cotton handkerchief. She was modestly attentive to him, and no longer shunned his gaze. He was gradually yielding to the temptation of braving another night in the hut, and seeing what would follow, when the old woman spoke.

"The weather will be broken all day, sir," she said. "You had better be going, or your friends will leave without you."

Ere he could answer, he saw such a beseeching glance on the face of the girl, that he hesitated, confused. Glancing at the mother, he saw the flash of wrath in her face. She rose and approached her daughter, with her hand lifted to strike her. The young woman stooped her head with a cry. He darted round the table to interpose between them. But the mother had caught hold of her; the handkerchief had fallen from her neck; and the youth saw five blue bruises on her lovely throat-the marks of the four fingers and the thumb of a left hand. With a cry of horror he darted from the house, but as he reached the door he turned. His hostess was lying motionless on the floor, and a huge gray wolf came bounding after him.

There was no weapon at hand; and if there had been, his inborn chivalry would never have allowed him to harm a woman even under the guise of a wolf. Instinctively, he set himself firm, leaning a little forward, with half outstretched arms, and hands curved ready to clutch again at the throat upon which he had left those pitiful marks. But the creature as she sprung eluded his grasp, and just as he expected to feel her fangs, he found a woman weeping on his bosom, with her arms around his neck. The next instant, the gray wolf broke from him, and bounded howling up the cliff. Recovering himself as he best might, the youth followed, for it was the only way to the moor above, across which he must now make his way to find his companions.

All at once he heard the sound of a crunching of bones-not as if a creature was eating them, but as if they were ground by the teeth of rage and disappointment; looking up, he saw close above him the mouth of the little cavern in which he had taken refuge the day before. Summoning all his resolution, he passed it slowly and softly. From within came the sounds of a mingled moaning and growling.

Having reached the top, he ran at full speed for some distance across the moor before venturing to look behind him. When at length he did so, he saw, against the sky, the girl standing on the edge of the cliff, wringing her hands. One solitary wail crossed the space between. She made no attempt to follow him, and he reached the opposite shore in safety.

GRAFFERS
[previously published on Anthrofiction;
winner of Winter 2010 Short Story Award]
Kadrian Blackwolf

Kadrian Blackwolf is just a regular guy who happens to love wolves and occasionally dabbles in writing. He enjoys furry fiction with characters that express some aspect of the animals they represent, hence the lecherous nature of the "wolf" in this story. Kadrian's first published work was "How Cruel the Wolf," on the Anthropomorphic Dreams website, July 2012. This is his second published work.

She was not surprised, after having met him in the woods, to find the wolf waiting for her at her grandfather's cottage. Nor was the absence of her ailing grandfather entirely unexpected considering what she had told the wolf during their conversation. Her grandfather—"Graffers," as he insisted she call him—had always been mean-spirited, demanding, and demeaning, and his debilitating illness had done nothing to improve his disposition. Therefore, it was with a certain satisfaction that she saw the door of the closet tightly closed and a heavy bench pushed up against it. The weekly treks to his cottage, burdened with the basket of food, braving rogues, brambles, and lately, prowling wolves, only to be rewarded with complaints and criticism, had long ago exhausted her patience. It was only because Graffers was too ill to go to the market himself that she was there at all.

So it was not entirely bad fortune when this particular wolf accosted her in the woods that morning. This *playful* wolf who had toyed with her by engaging her in casual conversation as he slowly stalked toward her, each measured step of his great paws bringing him closer until she could see every hair of his rough, disheveled coat. She held her ground and responded politely to his queries, telling him where she was going, how to get there, who was waiting for her, and the reason for the trip. She dared not take flight, she knew, for if she did the wolf would flatten her in an instant, and with nowhere to run, no place to hide, and no pearl-handled derringer tucked into her garter she could only wait and wonder when the terrible wolf would pounce and gobble her up.

Though she was surprised at the time—less surprised now, in light of recent developments—that wasn't what happened. Instead, the wolf stopped and studied her for a moment before turning his head to stare in the direction of her grandfather's cottage. His ears twitched as he gazed into the distance, and he appeared to be contemplating something she suspected she wanted to know nothing about. When he looked back at her, his muzzle boasted such an ungodly wolfishly wicked grin she was certain that even another wolf wouldn't want to know what this wolf was thinking about. But before her imagination could run away with itself, the wolf politely wished her a good day and bounded back into the woods, vanishing as suddenly as he had appeared.

She stared after him not fully believing he was actually gone and wondering if he would reappear in hopes of catching her off guard. But the wolf did not return, and after a minute or so, she realized she was holding her breath and collapsed to the ground with a gasp, panting and shaking uncontrollably while her heart pounded in her chest. When she had recollected her wits she sat on her basket, contemplating what had passed—and only then did it occur to her what she had done. "Oh, you wicked *bitch*," she whispered to herself.

She wanted to flee home, but she knew she could not for what was she to tell her mother? That she had seen a wolf that had done her no harm but whom she was certain had eaten Graffers? That was ridiculous. The wolf probably never went to Graffers' cottage at all, she told herself firmly, and Graffers was undoubtedly alive and waiting impatiently for his dinner. Yes, she would have to go to Graffers' cottage, but she would not go soon. She would wait for a while to give the wolf, if he was there, time to move on before she arrived. An hour or two should be enough—unless the wolf was planning on dessert.

Therefore, she was not surprised when Graffers failed to greet her with his usual, "You're late," or "Is it *fresh* this time?" or other welcoming remark. Nor was the presence of the wolf entirely unanticipated, for why should he settle for one bony old Graffers when he knew that the dutiful granddaughter would inevitably arrive, thus adding a plump Red Riding Hood to his catch? Even the condition of the cottage, rather than being a shambles with the shredded remains of Graffers lying on the floor, but instead looking cleaned and tidied in anticipation of her arrival, was not unexpected. After all, no predator worth his salt would allow some oversight to frighten away his prey. However, to find the wolf lying casually, even *seductively*, in Graffers' bed, fur carefully brushed and still damp from a recent bath, body clad in a nightshirt, and golden eyes gazing invitingly at her from beneath a stocking cap sitting awkwardly between his ears—now *that* was a surprise.

"Come in, my dear," said the wolf in what could almost be called a purr. "I was about to go looking for you."

Estimating how long it would take the wolf to leap from the bed to the door she concluded it would be somewhat less than the amount of time it would take for her to turn around in preparation for a quick departure. She slowly stepped inside and closed the door behind her. "My, what lovely *fur* you have, Graffers," she quipped.

The wolf lifted his head in a great basso laugh that rumbled like thunder in the tiny cottage. "And what a lovely gift for sardonicism you have, my dear," he replied, his jagged smile revealing his amusement. "Nonetheless, I am pleased by it. Now, do come closer so that I might have a look at you."

Having little alternative, she did as she was bid. She drew a nervous breath as the wolf leaned toward her, but he merely rested his cheek on one forepaw as he fixed his golden gaze upon her. "You are indeed a most refreshing change," he said with a touch of admiration. "In truth, I had already eaten my fill of venison and was only looking for a bit of amusement when I had the good fortune to cross paths with you in the forest. Most young ladies scream and run the moment they see me. You are the first to have allowed me to stalk so close without throwing stones or begging me to *pleeease* go away," he said with a grin.

Indeed, she was afraid of him, but his ready smile and easy laugh put her at ease, and she found herself looking him over as he lay in the bed. Actually, he looked rather charming lying there in that silly nightshirt, she thought. Too small to fit properly the front lay fully open, exposing the wolf's woolly torso from the ruff of his neck to the blanket pulled demurely over his hips. She bit her lip and composed herself. "I'm sorry if I disappointed you," she said dryly, determined to keep her unruly thoughts to herself.

"Oh, not at all, not at all!" the wolf laughed as he reached out to her with a massive forepaw. "If you had run away it would have been good for, at most, a minute or two of laughter, and then it would have been back to the usual dull day. I was quite gratified, even intrigued, when you refused to run, for with you lies the promise of far greater things."

Though she dreaded the wolf, she was intrigued by his fascination with her. She made no move to avoid him as he reached toward her, standing perfectly still even as he took the cord of her hood and deftly untied it. Being rather proud of her flowing red-blonde hair, she obliged the wolf, removing her hood and letting her wavy locks tumble about her shoulders. "Admittedly, I know nothing of wolves," she said hesitantly as the wolf withdrew his paw, "but I can't imagine why you would find me of interest."

The wolf regarded her for a long moment before he answered. "I find you of interest because wolves are creatures of the dark and *you* have a dark side to be sure. Exploring the darkness is perilous, but the rewards are decidedly worth the risk." He leaned closer and lowered his voice to a whisper as he brushed his paw lightly over her cheek. "You have the will to conquer your fears and the daring to do what others dare not. I am not one to pass by such a rare and wonderful creature as yourself without notice."

She felt the warmth of a blush touch her cheeks and looked down to her hands, folding her hood and dropping it on the basket. The wolf's powerful presence was enticing and she found herself spellbound by the sound of his voice when he whispered to her that way. "I didn't run from you because there was no point in it," she said quietly, still looking at her hands. "And if I have a dark side I haven't noticed it being particularly rewarding."

"And you are absolutely convinced of that, I'm sure," the wolf replied, moving his paw to gently lift her chin and gaze into her eyes. "As with most, you take the revealing light and turn it to blind yourself to your own nature. It is something you are taught to do from birth because only a precious few have the fortitude to see themselves as they truly are. You, however, are quite special, and if you will but grant me the pleasure of an evening with you, I will reveal to you the dark secret that you refuse to allow yourself to know." And with that, he lowered his paw to the lace of her bodice and smoothly untied it, the sound of the cord slipping over itself echoing from every wall.

The slight pop of the knot sent an indescribable sensation through her, and she drew her breath as the lace slipped through the grommets, her bodice loosening from around her. The wolf withdrew his paw and watched her expectantly, his expression wistful. Blushing once again at his interest, she raised her hands to her bodice and removed it, setting it on top of her hood. Gratified, the wolf smiled warmly and bid her to continue with a motion of his paw.

"I promised you a secret, and so I will tell you a simple one," the wolf said quietly as she began to unlace her boots. "Consider it an introduction; to perform some simple act while thinking about it in a particular way. Most people believe the light reveals with unadulterated clarity that which we see before us. In truth, we do what we will with the light, as often bending it into something we wish to see as blinding ourselves to what we do *not* wish to see. Indeed, you do it yourself, and most admirably I must say."

The stone floor was hard and cold on her bare feet. There was no fire. Graffers rarely made them, being too sick to collect the wood, letting the thick blankets and heavy comforter of his bed keep him warm. She gave the wolf a covetous gaze as she unfastened the buttons of her dress. "I'm pleased, I'm sure, but tell me, do you take such pains for every young woman you meet in the forest?"

"Only those I respect," he replied, his smile sincere. "But in truth, this is not a road I've traveled before, though it is one I have oft considered. Out of the countless dull and dreadful people that happen by, only a rare few have the boldness to approach a wolf. There are those who can appreciate the pleasures of what lies beyond the prescribed boundaries, and it is inevitable that one should occasionally have the good fortune to meet another."

The wolf's sonorous voice penetrated to the core of her being, resonating somewhere within her breast, his disarming dress and smooth words veiling in the softest of silk an evil she had never before imagined: evil solely for evil's sake. She slipped her arms from the sleeves of her dress and let it drop to the floor and then reached for the ties of her chemise, pulling them free. As the top of her chemise fell loosely about her shoulders, a tendril of doubt touched the edge of her mind. Could this be a jest? Having failed to get a rise out of her in the forest was he now luring her into some other twisted game? If she refused him, would he let her go or would she find herself keeping company with Graffers until the wolf's appetite returned? She crossed her arms over her breast, holding the chemise in place as she looked to the wolf, trying to read his expression in the masked pattern of his face.

Sensing her doubt, the wolf sat up and reached out to her, taking her by the shoulders and looking into her eyes. "Your grandfather was a miserable and demanding old nuisance that you wanted out of your life," he whispered softly but firmly to her, "and though you lacked the wherewithal to kill him yourself you nonetheless dispatched him with the swiftness and certainty of any wolf."

She gasped in horror at the accusation and opened her mouth to protest, but the wolf touched a silencing paw to her lips and shook his head. "Oh, no, no, of course you didn't realize—or didn't intend, or didn't want, or didn't whatever it is that you are assuring yourself that you didn't do," he continued, putting his paws around her waist as he spoke. "But as sure as I occupy this bed while your grandfather does not, *you did it.*"

Again she tried to protest but she found herself unable to speak, her denials ringing false and empty even to herself, her words melting before the terrible secret, the terrible *truth* the wolf had revealed to her. His eyes burned into the depths of her being, illuminating thoughts so dark she scarcely believed they dwelt within her. She closed her eyes, sobbing with the full realization of what she had done.

"Oh, you *wonderfully* wicked bitch!" declared the wolf with admiration, his voice surrounding her as she stood helpless in his embrace. He knew. He *knew!* she realized as he echoed her own words. "Why would it take you two hours to arrive when this cottage is no more than a half hour's distance from where we spoke? Why did you sit calmly soaking your feet in the river rather than running for help in the hopes that you might save your poor grandfather's life? Because you knew what you wanted and you knew that I would provide it; all you had to do was allow the seed *you* planted to come to fruition."

She sobbed uncontrollably while he held her, lovingly caressing her and whispering softly to her. In time, she put her arms around the wolf's shoulders and embraced him, her chemise dropping unnoticed to her feet.

"Poor dear," the wolf said in his smoothest purr. "You surely must be freezing. Come, join me in this wonderful bed, and allow me to show you that I am not entirely rough and course."

"My God," she whispered in a voice that shook from her innermost depths. "Then you truly *do* want me in bed with you?"

"My dear lady," replied the wolf as he guided her into the warm depths of the blankets, "you've been in bed with me from the moment we met in the forest."

The light of dawn found her awake in Graffers' bed. The air was bitter cold and lay like a mask of ice upon her face, while the bed was deep and warm and she was loath to leave its comfort. The wolf was, as he had promised, not all rough and course. But though his pleasures had made her blush to the roots of her hair, it was clear that the pleasures he sought most were his own, and her time might be measured in minutes; she did not wish to be nearby when the wolf awakened.

Carefully, she slipped her feet out from under the blankets and over the edge of the bed, shivering as the frigid air wrapped itself around them. Sitting up slowly, she turned to look at the wolf: he slept silently, his breathing slow and even. She eased herself out of the bed and as she bent to retrieve her chemise the closet caught her eye. From behind the door came a dozen dark rivulets that stained the woodwork a hideous color before congealing on the floor in a glistening black pool.

"Leaving so soon, my love?" The wolf spoke softly, but his voice boomed in the deathly silence of the cottage. She choked back a scream and ransacked her mind for a likely excuse before an urgent need inspired a truthful response.

"I fear that I must," she whispered, trying desperately to hide the terror in her voice, "otherwise that cozy bed will not remain cozy for much longer."

"Ah, of course," the wolf replied drowsily, "though do hurry back."

She held her chemise tightly in front of her, deciding to wait until she was safely out of the cottage before putting it on; she wished to leave as quickly as possible, before the wolf came to his senses. As she stepped outside and into the stinging cold, she took a last glance at the wolf before closing door quietly behind her.

Walking as softly as she could, her bare feet protesting the frozen ground, she hoped that the wolf would not notice that her footsteps receded towards the woods rather than the privy. When she was certain she was beyond his hearing, she picked up her pace, changing first to a hasty walk and then a dead run toward home.

She ran holding her chemise before her, still afraid that the wolf would awaken and realize she was escaping him. Twice she thought she heard him behind her, but when she turned to look there was nothing to see. Fearing that he was shadowing her by running just out of sight in the woods, she increased her pace, running full speed until her ankle was seized in an unbreakable grip.

She saw the ground rise up to meet her and screamed in pain and terror as she slammed into the frozen ground. She covered her head with her arms, trying to protect herself even though she knew she was defenseless against the terrible wolf. She waited anxiously for the first crushing bite and the penetration of his fangs as he shredded her flesh, but the wolf did not attack. When at last she looked over her shoulder, there was nothing behind her save an upturned root that she had failed to see in her headlong flight.

Scrambling to her feet, she left her chemise behind, running in blind panic as her suppressed fear came bursting to the surface. She tore headlong though the forest, mindless of all that was before her, knowing only of the horror that was behind her. Rocks bruised her feet, branches scratched her face, and canes whipped her thighs and belly, but she was barely aware of them, feeling only the terror she sought to escape.

Behind her, the dark figure of the wolf stood in the open doorway of the cottage, ears pricked and nose glistening. He heard the pounding of her feet, her sobbing breath, the sounds of her fall, her cries of pain, and the slap of every limb against her flesh. He smelled her fear, her sweat, and even the remnants of her passion as it came wafting to him on the chill morning breeze, but though his instincts were strong, he did not give chase. When, at length, she was finally beyond his senses, he smiled and spoke softly after her: "Today a nibble, tomorrow a bite, until little by little, bit by bit, I shall devour you."

GLASS
[previously published in the Camp Feral conbook]
Slip Wolf

Slip Wolf is a wolf because there is no world in which he would be anything else. He's grey, reasonably kempt and smells healthy. He rolls in story ideas and seeks guidelines to gnaw on, howling at bright, hallow editorial inboxes by night. But there's nothing wrong with him. This is his nature.

It's dark where we are, and I have it trapped. My skin sings with the sweat on it as I gaze into the beast's eyes, glints of menace over a muzzle curling back from razor teeth. The wolf doesn't hammer at its prison's glass wall. It merely stares daggers at me. I don't know whether it's given up or biding its time, ignorant of the finality of this moment.

"I have you, son of a bitch," I spit at it. "Your reign of terror is now and forever at an end."

"Nope." It shakes its shaggy head. "I've just begun."

I bare my flat teeth back at the bastard, leaning forward until my nose nearly touches the prison's skin. "You've killed your last camper, you spawn from hell. I've seen what you did to the hikers on that trail. I followed your leavings back to the boys in the shower. I even found the remains you left under the dock where the kids swim every day. Your evil has permeated every fiber of this place for too long, preying on the weak, the drunk, the ignorant—"

"Don't forget the lechery," the creature adds proudly, the fur rising and falling on its naked chest. Its breath fogs the unbreakable barrier. "The lust of these debauched souls…It draws me back time and time again. I love that more than anything." It purses its lips in the start of a howl, and its dark nose twitches as though smelling blood in the air.

I batter furiously at the wall next to the glass barrier between us. The creature starts, ears dropping low, lips pulling back in a growl. "Never again!" I shout triumphantly. I finally had a prison it would never escape, painstakingly crafted by my own hand. "It's taken years, but the world is free of you at last."

The wolf's laughter freezes my blood as it shakes its great head. "Would it surprise you to know that I've heard those words before? Always the promise that my fun in this camp is over. And always wrong." It sniffs. "So, tell me, how did you build this prison exactly?"

I scoff. "Like I'm going to give you a hope in hell of figuring out how to escape."

The creature shrugs, muscles rippling under its pelt. "But of course you won't. You've worked so hard to put me 'here.' Answer me this then: whose stomach is growling right this moment?"

The low rumble of hunger erupts deep inside me, but I push it down, mercilessly. More tricks. More distractions. The creature's options have run out, and all it has left are meaningless diversions. This prison will hold it. I know it will. It has to.

But I have to understand. "You're a monster without even a soul. How the hell do you know what I'm feeling?"

I raise my hand to rap insistently on the hot fogged glass and the wolf raises its paw with me, mocking me through mimicry. Its paw is bare but for its claws. The razor, as it turns out, is in my hand.

"Just shut up," it chuckles. "And finish shaving."

A WINTER'S WORK
[previously published in *Renard's Menagerie* (7), 2008]
Renee Carter Hall

Renee Carter Hall works as a medical transcriptionist by day and as a writer all the time. Her short fiction and poetry have appeared in a variety of publications both inside and outside the furry fandom, including Strange Horizons, Daily Science Fiction, Podcastle, *and the anthologies* Bewere the Night, ROAR, An Anthropomorphic Century, *and* Wolf Warriors III. *While admittedly more of a cat person, she included a wolf tribe in her novel* By Sword and Star *and admires wolves for their supportive social relationships and their varied roles in myth and folklore. Readers can find Renee online at www.reneecarterhall.com and on Twitter as @RCarterHall.*

January, 1829

    My dear Emma,

    As I write these words, the snow is deep and drifting around my tent, and more is falling, but I keep my ink near the candle-flame to keep it from freezing, and I keep myself warm with thoughts of you.

    It has been a good winter thus far, and when at last I leave these mountains to return to you in the spring, I hope to earn enough to start a home for us. The glossy mink I caught only yesterday should fetch enough in cloth to make you a wedding dress fine as any city girl's.

    A night like this is too cold and wild for sleep, so I fall to dreaming instead. I think of the day you will be my wife. I think of the home we will have together, and the children who will come to fill our arms and light our days. In my mind, the tiny flame that lights this tent becomes a warm hearth, and we sit before it together for the rest of our lives, and I know there is no man on earth richer than I...

By morning the storm had broken, and he packed up and moved camp downriver, checking his traps along the way, rejoicing at the full ones and giving the resolute shrug of the faithful to the ones he found empty. He found one trap that seemed deliberately sprung, and on searching found the fine-fingered pawprints of the raccoon. Other men might have sworn, but he chuckled. Even though he lived by the beasts, lived by their deaths, he loved them in a way he could not put into words. There was a kind of understanding between them, he thought, and he respected it.

As winter's early evening darkened the sky, he built a fire and spitted two rabbits for his dinner, then read his letter to Emma over again while they cooked. Perhaps he could find someone at the trading post who could carry it along to town, but likely he'd reach her again himself before the letter ever did. Still, it was a comfort to talk to her, even if only on the few scraps of paper he'd saved from his supplies.

He tucked the letter away and looked up to see a figure standing at the edge of the firelight, a pale gray pelt against the blue-shadowed snow.

He tensed and reached for his rifle. He did not raise it, but the cold metal under his fingertips allowed him enough reassurance to be able to think. He had heard stories of the wolfen at the trading posts and forts, tales told at the firesides of lonely cabins—but he had never seen one before.

They were not always dangerous, the stories held. Especially not when they were alone. But a man had to be careful out on his own. A pack could hide easily in these woods, unseen until the right moment...

It came closer. It walked in a hesitant half-crouch, stealing forward, then cringing back. The smell of the roasting meat had drawn it, he figured. It was close enough now that he could make out the ears held erect, the slope of the muzzle, and the hands with their padded fingertips and dark nails.

Closer still. It was trembling, he saw now--from cold or weakness, he couldn't tell. Then it edged full into the fire's glow, and he blinked in surprise.

It, he saw now, was a she, her breasts full and hanging, the dark nipples wet. Her eyes were pale gold, the color of new honey, and she was so thin that every bone poked an angle under her silver-gray fur. She wore only a scrap of skin tied about her waist—rabbit, he noted—and he wondered if it had some purpose as a sign of rank or place, as it did nothing to cover the vague cleft between her legs.

He had heard they had a language, a kind of growling, yipping speech accented with posture and signs. He knew none of it. All he could do was force himself not to stare, afraid it might provoke her.

After a moment, though, he realized there was no need to worry on that point. Her own attention was focused solely on the meat as it dripped its juices into the sizzling fire. He saw her salivate, saw the hollow of her belly.

44

Rabbits were thin this time of year, but one would be enough to keep him until morning. He took the meat from the spit, singeing his fingers in the process, and held one of the rabbits out to her.

"Take it," he said, keeping his voice low. "It's all right."

She flinched back at the sound of his voice, but the meat was impossible to resist. She snatched the rabbit from him, retreated to the edge of the fire, and tore into the meat. It was gone in a few moments, and he heard the bones cracking between her teeth.

He glanced at her chest again. Had she been human, he would never have dared, but he found that her nudity didn't even register as such. She was nursing, so that meant there were pups in a den nearby. Given her current state, it was a wonder she still had milk to give.

He took a haunch from the second rabbit—hesitated— then held the rest out to her. She took it as eagerly as the first, though he noticed she ate it more slowly. When she was done, only the clean, tooth-scarred bones remained.

Now that the food was gone, he expected her to leave, but instead she stayed by the fire, inspecting him with frank curiosity. He wondered if she had ever seen a human before. So few people came into these mountains, and the wolfen were known to keep to themselves.

Her gaze fell then on his pack, and she approached it gingerly, sniffing at it as a hound might. Then she pulled back a bit, and her eyes darkened.

The pack's ties gave her a little trouble, but soon she had it open. She lifted out his last steel trap, the one he hadn't had time to set before sundown. She held it, turning it this way and that in the firelight, sniffing it, touching it with her tongue, running her fingers over it, all as if searching for something.

Then she stood and flung the trap far into the woods. He did not hear it fall into the snow.

———

She returned to the pack, focusing now on the tied bundles of furs, cutting their bindings with her teeth, rummaging through them, smelling them, tossing them aside. He winced at all his careful work undone but made no move to stop her. What was she looking for?

At last, when all his furs lay scattered in the snow, she slumped to her knees, head low, eyes closed. A low sound came from deep in her throat, half whine and half sigh.

He knew nothing of wolfen speech, but he didn't need words to understand the weariness, the hopelessness in the haggard line of her body. This was not mere physical weakness, he knew; this was the weight of sorrow.

And then he knew what she must have been looking for, and he fought a rise of hot bile in his throat.

He had once heard another trapper say that the wolfen pups fetched good money for their hides, if you could get them young enough, if you could take them from the den while the bitch was away—their fur, he was told, was so fine and soft, it was just the thing for rich ladies' gloves...

He must have made a sound, because she turned her empty eyes to him.

"Your pups," he said softly, holding his arms to mimic cradling a child.

She looked down, then after a moment, slowly raised her head again to look at him, her eyes searching his.

"No," he said. "I wouldn't. I couldn't."

She seemed to understand. At last she stood and trudged through the snow, out of the fire's warm circle. He wanted to call her back somehow, but he didn't. Instead, he watched her disappear into the dark trees, and hours later, when he heard her howls rise into the bitter air, he could not have said if she was mourning for her lost young, or for herself.

He looked up from the account-books as the two men entered the store: Rafe the trapper, stinking of whiskey as usual, and behind him, Henrik from upriver. Henrik had a new young wife, he'd heard, and he smiled to see the burly logger fingering the ribbons and the calico goods.

Rafe dropped a bundle of furs onto the counter. "And I want what I'm due," he said. "There's hides here worth their weight in gold."

He nodded absently in reply and sorted through the pelts, keeping a tally on a bit of paper. Mink, beaver, raccoon, fox... In his mind, he saw each creature as it must have been while still alive, so fleet and cunning and whole. For his part, he preferred the store work now, except when the sun slanted in and hit the jars of wild honey so they glowed on the dusty shelves.

Then his fingers brushed a scrap of pale gray.

He swallowed. His vision went black at the edges, and a high-pitched buzzing droned suddenly in his ears. He fought to keep his voice from shaking. "And this one is...?"

Rafe grinned. "Best of the lot. Only got the one—the bitch made off with the other. Shame we can't hunt the big ones too. She'd have made a fine rug, that one."

The buzzing in his ears became a roar, and the next thing he knew, Henrik was holding him back while Rafe laughed.

He struggled, but the logger's grip was firm. "Don't," Henrik said in his ear. "Don't, hear me? You don't need trouble. Think about Emma. Think about William."

Oh, but William was all he could think of—his own baby boy, his skin so soft, his eyes still opening up to everything around him. Had that pup's eyes been open yet?

Rafe was gone. He felt Henrik release him at last, and he staggered out of the store into the melting snow.

The town was still and silent, and he imagined he could hear it. Somewhere high in the mountains, there would be another bitch—

Another woman—

—singing her heart's death-song to an empty sky.

Wind chilled the tears on his cheeks. He threw back his head and howled.

THE WINTER WOLF
[previously published in *Wolf Warriors III: Winter Wolves*]
Kristen Hubschmid

When she's not writing, KHub works in the film industry on shows like Wynonna Earp and Fargo, or on commercials in her local town as a videographer. Her debut novel, **The Meddler,** *is coming to the world in 2017, featuring idealistic freshman Reo, who strays into a criminal underworld, where only a quick wit and courage will get her out alive. Check out khubswindow.com for more!*

"Be careful, Carter. You've heard how they settle things out there. I'm not gonna buy a pair of those knee-high clodhoppers and sod through some forsaken forest, looking for your tooth fillings with a metal detector, got me?"

Carter adjusted the phone against his shoulder in order to navigate the overpass that would take him off Highway 2, plunging him through the ankles of a looming evergreen forest. The late fall sunlight warming his short golden fur flickered and disappeared. Towering trees reared up on either side, squeezing the blue sky into a narrow crack overhead.

"Did you get the deed from that South Bettony pub…what's it called…"

"Don't change the subject. Listen to this: 'business magnate goes missing on Christmas holiday in James Falls.' 'Insurance broker last seen in James Falls during snowstorm.'"

"Bev, most of these wolf packs have never even seen a city lawyer, much less learned to outwit one. Would you relax?" He checked his watch. Seventy minutes to go on this winding, cracked pavement. How the mountain village of James Falls drew so much summer tourism, he didn't know. The drive alone was enough to discourage *him*, but he knew the numbers. They'd have retreated back to the city by this time, but in the days between May and October, tourists outnumbered the local wolf pack a hundred to one. Which was why the village bar— he cast a quick glance at the paperwork on the seat beside him—Knothole Pub—was flourishing so spectacularly, the fame of its wild game menu increasing with every summer.

"They don't need to outwit a lawyer. Just you," Bev snapped. "Don't lose focus. The minute you lose focus, we're done, understand?"

"Yeah, yeah."

"Check in with me after they've signed."

"Yep."

Carter tapped End Call and tossed the phone on the leather passenger seat beside his wallet and a thick folder of papers.

The radio gave him only static, as expected. He'd already made the drive three times to speak with Adel, one of the owners of the Knothole, but this should be his last trip out. He glanced at the folder, feeling a wave of satisfaction. Last trip.

The immense trees marched by on either side like sentinels, all but the foremost trunks obscured by thick green foliage. He was prepared for it, but the narrowness of the road and the height of the stretching branches seemed to compress him on either side, squeezing in as though to stifle him. His foot leaned heavier on the gas pedal.

Finally, the village of James Falls came into view, appearing suddenly through the trees where there was nothing a moment before. Carter hit the brakes, careening into the parking lot with more speed than he intended, and lurched to a halt in front of the rough-lumber veranda.

Knothole Pub reared up to the sky, a wide wooden peak supported by twisting, gnarled tree-trunk columns. Carved into the columns, the faces of a dozen ferocious-looking wolves leered in frozen malice, or watched him with quiet suspicion. He supposed they were part of the allure of this place, but he was considering the cost of sanding them off.

The wooden faces didn't discourage visitors, however. In the warmer months, tourists normally thronged the capacious wrap-around veranda. But now, though it was only late October, pine needles lay in windblown dunes on the tables, and spiderwebs sparkled everywhere. This past summer had not gone well for the pub, as he knew better than most.

Carter gathered up the folder, along with his wallet and phone. A rumbling sound echoed off the trees, growing louder as Carter checked the cell service bars. The village had its own cell tower, and he should be able to call Bev easily once he'd completed his business here.

As he stuck one foot out the door of his car, the source of the rumbling sound made itself apparent. A pickup rolled into the lot to park beside Carter, a pickup the likes of which he had never seen. No one in the city drove anything remotely like it; you'd never find a parking space big enough to fit into, and he suspected it would break the noise restriction bylaw in his neighborhood. He doubted, however, that either of those problems were ever an issue. Judging by the mud caked on the tires, it wasn't a truck that spent much time on pavement, let alone on city streets.

Carter stepped out of the car into a cloud of diesel fumes. The breeze quickly whisked them away, but his annoyance remained. He walked around the back of the truck to have a word, but as he passed the bumper, something arrested his eye.

A trickle of blood dripped from the tailgate, pattering softly to the pavement, and in the guttering breeze he caught a sudden powerful whiff of its metallic scent.

The pickup door opened. A ragged boot, something like the 'clodhoppers' Bev had mentioned, kicked caked mud to the sidewalk before its owner jumped down to the pavement. He had to be four or five inches taller than Carter, and Carter was not short—as an Anatolian Shepherd, he outsized most people he met. But this wolf loomed over him, his yellow eyes vivid against the varied grays framing his face and neck.

Carter found his tongue somewhat stuck. He made to continue on to the door, as though walking around the back of the pickup had been an arbitrary decision.

"You'd better make sure that fancy car doesn't stay here too long."

The wolf, scraping a last bit of mud from his heavy boots, shut the truck door and strode directly toward Carter.

"Pardon me?" Carter said, halting. The wolf passed him, leaving mingled scents of wood smoke and spruce swirling in his wake, and opened his tailgate with considerable wrenching. He dragged a rough wooden crate from the box of the truck, catching his shredded jacket sleeve on a corner and ripping it further.

"I said you'd better leave with that fancy car before long," the wolf said, his yellow eyes steady. "Snow's coming, and those Mickey Mouse tires won't get you far."

Carter cast a glance at the sky. It was still blue, fading toward evening indigo, but blue nonetheless.

"I shouldn't be here long," Carter said, turning to continue on his way.

"Could you give me a hand, here?" The wolf pulled a second crate onto the tailgate. "I need to bring both of these in."

Carter surveyed the crates. "What's in them?"

"A moose."

"*A moose?* In those two little crates?"

"You can fit a lot of meat in these, if you cut it up right."

Carter beheld the crates with a sense of incredulity. It seemed too incredible that packed in those crates were the parts of a feral creature, recently living but now sliced up into edible portions. He had never really given such things much thought, having been raised in the suburbs. He hefted the heavy folder, the pages fluttering slightly in the breeze.

"This is an extremely important agreement, sir—I hope you don't mind if I just head inside. I have business with the owners of this pub."

"Head inside with one of these," the wolf said, thrusting one of the crates at Carter. The silence hung, the wolf's yellow gaze fixed unblinkingly on Carter's face. Finally, Carter placed the folder carefully on top of the crate before taking it.

"Have...have these crates come very far, unrefrigerated?" Carter asked.

"They've been properly cooled," the wolf growled. He led the way up the veranda's uneven steps, each one a tree trunk split in half and worn smoothest in the center.

"Excellent...excellent," Carter said. "Do you always bring the game for the menu?" It would soon be his concern, if things went as expected this evening.

The wolf shrugged. "If I have business down here, I do."

"You don't live in the area?"

The wolf held the door for Carter with his elbow.

"I'm only here for the night," the wolf replied. "After my business is finished here, I'll go back up the mountain."

The noise of voices spilling out the open door was not what Carter had anticipated; the previous trips had brought him into a silent room, empty but for the owner. Inside, after his eyes finally adjusted to the low light, he realized nearly the whole village had to be here. Wolves of every size lounged on barstools, pinning him in the crosshairs of thirty yellow-eyed glares.

Conversation lulled, and Carter felt the pressure of those gazes sweeping over his ice-white dress shirt, his business slacks paired with gleaming shoes, his Gartier watch, and his styled hair. None of them looked as though they'd ever heard of trimming their hair, let alone styling it. Some wore paint on their faces in bright blues or reds; according to urban researchers, symbols of some kind of spiritual accomplishment. Thick smoke from several pipes hazed the air, reeking of something earthy and sharp. Carter's eyes began to water. He coughed loudly and followed the wolf to the bar, where they deposited their crates of moose meat.

The barman, Adel, appeared before them, spinning a rag over a pint glass.

"This one's healthy, then?" he asked the wolf coolly, glancing at the crates.

Carter paused in the midst of inspecting the folder of papers, his eyes drawn by a slight change in the air between the Adel and the gray wolf. They had shifted, as though into a stand-off, face to face over the bar.

"I've told you before," the wolf said quietly. "Every animal I bring you is healthy."

"Apparently not every one," Adel replied curtly. He, like Carter, was much shorter than the gray wolf, and his white fur nearly gleamed in the half-light. In the common custom of wolves, he'd had a permanent tattoo dyed into the roots of his hair, a sleeve of black twisting markings almost entirely covering his right arm.

Snatching a folded newspaper from between two whiskey bottles, Adel flung it on the counter before the gray wolf.

"Seen this?"

The gray wolf's eyes darted over the front page article.

"'Local pub loses everything in food-disease scare'," Adel quoted. "Looks like everyone in the country has heard about it."

"It's not right!" snapped an elderly wolf seated at the bar, clapping his tumbler against the wood. "I've never heard of this 'wasting disease'—how do they know she got sick from our food, eh? How do they know that?"

"They don't have to prove it, boss," the barman growled, snatching the newspaper and tossing it in a nearby garbage bin. "She ate our food, she got sick. It's enough to scare folk off."

The gray wolf left the bar, skirting the edge of the room, and found a seat at one of the empty tables in the back, where he flagged the waitress.

"You shouldn't have gone to court about it," said an older female seated beside the first elderly wolf. "Shouldn't have made a stink."

"What's done is done!" Adel cried. "Had to try and prove ourselves innocent, didn't we?"

"Didn't help you none, did it?" the female wolf hissed.

"Please, friends!" Carter said, raising his voice above the babble sweeping through the pub. "I know you've been through hard times this past summer. I know lawyers aren't cheap!"

They stabbed him with their multitude of gazes again. He had not been prepared to speak to a room of wolves, but he could improvise. This may be a chance to smooth things over.

He continued. "I'm here to give you all another chance to succeed." A flurry of mutterings went through them at this. "I'm buying this pub to keep it in business, and keep dollars in local pockets. We can get your good reputation back. We can bring people back."

Carter held the folder of papers up, turning back to the barman and the elderly wolf. "I just need the signatures of the two owners to close the sale, and we're in business."

The barman regarded him coolly. "Well. I'm sure I need to read through those papers before I sign anything."

This was as Carter expected. He scanned the bar quickly, but there appeared to him no one that suited the description of lawyer. It seemed Adel had neglected to hire an expert to oversee the buyer's agreement, which suited Carter just fine.

"Should we retire to your office, then?"

Adel pierced him with a look. "No, I'm gonna read it right here."

Carter gave a polite nod. "If you'd like some time, I think I'll order some of your famous food. Can I try the Smoked Barbeque Burger?"

Adel took the folder of papers from him, giving him a glare through narrowed eyes.

"Sure, Mr. Carter. We can make whatever you want."

Carter sat himself at the last open barstool. "Excellent."

"For the purchase of the aforementioned property—" Adel began to read, his voice overcoming the low bubble of conversation.

"Mr. Adel," Carter said sharply. "Are you planning to read *aloud* from the agreement? I would not advise it…privacy is your right."

Adel gave him a long glare. "These here are concerned citizens, Carter. And I will read aloud so all shareholders can hear. Got it?"

Shareholders, Carter thought derisively. These were stakeholders, not shareholders. Only the two owners could be properly called 'shareholders'. But if they didn't know the difference between such things out here, so much the better—incidentally, that was a large part of why he and Bev had chosen this place.

Adel proceeded to read out great swaths of the buyer agreement, speaking on from the delivery of Carter's meal through to his dessert (maple grillcake, an old lupine recipe), stopping to re-read whenever a random wolf requested it. The elderly wolf he'd referred to as "boss" nodded off at times and was poked sharply back to awareness by his mate, blinking repeatedly.

Carter watched it all with increasing contentment. The listeners frequently struggled with long words, many of them calling for Adel to move on before an understanding was reached. Ridiculous, their disinterest in understanding how or why ownership would be transferred to Carter (or rather, Midland Holdings, whom he represented). It was just as well none of them lived in the city. They'd never survive it. They assumed the contract was fair and correct when they couldn't understand it, and yet made a show of checking its validity.

Carter sipped the amber ale he'd ordered. At least they knew their beer. It was excellent stuff, smooth and rich, and served in a chilled glass. They brewed it here in the village. Perhaps, he'd think about acquiring the brewery, once he'd solidified his foothold here.

"That's it," Adel said finally, flipping the last page of the contract. "Now, there's two places to sign. Does anyone have anything more to say?"

The pub was silent, more likely because several of the wolves had fallen asleep on their tables, than because they were satisfied with the agreement.

Carter produced a pen. "If you're in agreement with the contract, then I'll need you two to sign."

Adel took the pen and scrawled his signature on the space labeled B. *Adel* without hesitation.

"And yourself, sir?" Carter said, turning to the elderly wolf.

"Myself?" the wolf asked him, shaking his shaggy head.

"Yes, sir," Carter said smoothly. "I need the signatures of both owners."

The old wolf stared at him as though trying to pull him into focus. "I'm not the owner." He stared for another moment and began to chuckle. "I'm not the owner, sonny. I've no Adel blood in me."

Carter felt the eyes of all the wolves again, a roll of chuckles running through the room.

"But Adel called you boss, did he not?"

"Ah, that's just what they call me," the old wolf barked in a rough laugh. "I'm an elder! Didn't you see my face on the lee pillar out there?" He raised a gnarled hand, pointing out to the veranda.

In an effort to cut the tide of smirking from his vision, Carter swung his gaze back to Adel.

"You told me I would get both signatures."

"You will," Adel agreed, sliding Carter's empty plate into a rubber bin for washing. "This here says I have twenty-four hours to sign, right?"

"Yes—"

"Well, so long as everything is ship-shape with the winter wolf, you'll have both signatures before this time tomorrow. Another pint, boss?"

"If it please yeh."

Adel swept the empty pint glass away and turned to the towers of clean ones, glittering beside the line of draught taps.

"The winter wolf?" Carter demanded. "And who might that be?"

"Bit of a legend around here," Adel told him nonchalantly, his eyes fixed on the patient creation of a foamless pint. "Anything big goes on around here, you make sure you ask him about it. But I stopped believing in that when I was seven."

"Stopped believing!" the old wolf's mate cried. "Watch your tongue, son. He'll bring the snow if you're not careful!" Again, snickers and mutterings shivered through the attendant audience, rising to a head at the back of the room.

Adel slid the golden-hued pint across the counter, shooting an amused look that way.

"Like I said. So long as no one has any more to say on the matter, we'll leave it up to the winter wolf for the night." He swept the room with a glance. Only silence greeted his words, though a few of the wolves shifted restlessly.

"I'd say it's a family matter now," the wolf elder said, sipping his pint with well-practiced appreciation.

"All right, then we all agree," Adel said, depositing the folder of papers on the back counter with a slap.

"Adel, I was not prepared for—" Carter began, getting to his feet.

"If it's a bed and a toothbrush you need, we have an inn. Gerty keeps it wonderfully, don't you Gerty?"

The wolf elder's mate nodded sanctimoniously. "As nice as these hands can muster."

"There you are, Carter," Adel said. "A chance to keep the dollars in local pockets."

Carter stood up quickly. "I am not prepared to stay the night. I'm not sure what the delay is, you had plenty of time to alert your co-owner." He cast a glance around the pub and found nearly the entire pack had followed him to his feet. "But...I will return tomorrow morning."

The sudden buzz of his cell phone gave him an opportunity to avoid their unflinching gazes.

"This is Carter," he said. "How can I help you?"

"Well?" In that one syllable, Bev's impatience was evident. "What's taking so long? Have they signed it over to you yet?"

Carter turned away from the rest of the bar. "I'm with one of the owners now."

"And?"

"I'll update you on my drive home. Not now." He tapped End Call sharply.

The wolves still watched him, though they'd subsided into quiet conversation with each other. The only one who had not stood was the gray wolf at the back table. Ignoring the rest of the bar's inhabitants, he left a couple bills and strode out the door.

After the company had watched him exit, Adel signaled them all to sit down with an impatient wave of his dishtowel.

"All right. Mr. Carter said he'll be back in the morning, didn't he?"

Carter paid for his meal and took his leave with the promise of returning at noon tomorrow. He left the parking lot empty despite the number of wolves gathered there, and set out on the road toward the city, muttering aloud.

"...can't believe these barbarians. And people love them for it! Unbelievable..."

Potholes veered at him left and right out of the darkness. He swerved through with ease, having by this time learned the location of the worst of them.

He didn't notice the climb of his engine temperature dial until it beeped shrilly at him.

"What?" he growled at the offending warning light.

It shrilled again and began to flash. Smoke licked from the edges of the car hood, shadowy against the illuminated pavement.

Carter guided the car onto the side of the road, the beeping continuing without pause until he wrenched the key out. The rushing hiss seemed loud against the sudden silence of the engine.

"*What?!*" Carter muttered, staring at the dashboard with his hands in the air. He knew nothing about cars. Nothing. This one was only a year old, purchased brand new when he and Bev had acquired Fry Guys (makers of the legendary 'sour cream poutine').

The silent road stretched before Carter nearly a kilometer before it twisted and disappeared. Behind, it sloped up into the alpine valley Knothole Pub nestled in, but nowhere was there any break in the trees, or any hint of a nearby habitation.

As the hiss from under the hood waned, other noises began to filter into Carter's consciousness. Flanking him like bookends, the trembling trees hid the source of a continuous scraping and rustling. Every now and then, a sharp crack would sound, as though someone snapped a branch over their knee not fifty feet away. Other sounds punctured the general rustle; hoots and bugles and twitters, some echoing from a distance, some seemingly from a few steps away.

Carter wrested the owner's manual from his cluttered glovebox, flipping through the index.

"Smoke. Smoke? What happens if there's smoke?"

A low, growling noise filtered through the car's closed windows. Jerking, Carter surveyed the surroundings, eyes leaping from tree trunk to tree trunk.

The growling increased in intensity until he recognized the sound. Headlights blazed on the road behind him, beaming down the slope. It was the gray wolf's truck, trundling down the potholed road.

At least it wasn't his tires that had him stuck here. Mickey Mouse tires, had the wolf said?

Carter put his flashers on, sending blooms of yellow light over the trees as the truck crept to a stop a few feet from his back bumper.

Carter climbed out of his car as a black silhouette crossed through the truck headlights.

"Hello!" he cried. "I was wondering if I'd see anyone on this road!"

The gray wolf made no reply, but he stopped in front of Carter, surveying him.

"It's smoking from under the hood," Carter added, quelling a strange urge to keep talking.

"Did you have a look?"

Carter balked. "Um, not yet."

"Is the hood popped?"

"Uh…" Carter descended to the driver's seat and scanned the interior. "I've never needed to open it before…"

The wolf walked round to the front bumper, hands in his pockets.

No button presented itself. Carter seized the owner's manual. Surely it would tell him where the hood release was. He flipped madly through a few pages before the breeze grabbed them and spun through a third of the book—

The wolf reached suddenly past him, pulling on a small lever by his foot that looked nothing like a lever—Carter hadn't even heard him move.

Casting him an unreadable look, the wolf returned to the front of the car and opened the hood. A waft of smoke mushroomed out.

Carter followed, peering at the spidery mess of tubes and wires that made up his car's engine. It was unintelligible to him. The wolf leaned against the open hood, clearly waiting for him to comment. Finally, he broke the silence.

"Do you see where your problem is?"

Carter blinked between him and the engine. "Um."

"Your coolant line is cut." In the silence that greeted these words, he seemed compelled to add, "Your engine overheated because you have no coolant."

"Ah," Carter nodded. "Can that be fixed?"

The wolf regarded him for another long moment. "I have some electrical tape in my truck."

"Good…that's…excellent."

Pushing off the hood, the wolf strode back to his pickup. After some moments of rummaging, he dropped a jug of what Carter assumed was coolant on the pavement and shut the truck door. He stood, pausing by the box of his truck. Apparently making a decision, he dragged out a large wooden crate, this one empty, and dropped it on the pavement. He dropped something else on top—perhaps a hunting knife?—encased in leather.

Leaving those items where they lay, the wolf returned with the jug and a roll of black tape.

"This should be enough for you to make it to the city," the wolf said, setting the jug down. He donned a pair of darkly stained leather gloves before leaning carefully over the engine, poking and prodding at some sort of tubing.

"I thought you'd want to stay in James Falls. Keep the dollars in their pockets."

Carter felt a flutter of annoyance. "I thought you were headed back up the mountain? Find some more big game?"

"Plenty of game around here." He seemed to locate what he was looking for, and peeled a strip of tape from the roll with his teeth. With care, he wrapped it several times around the coolant line, re-sealing the clean slice in the rubber.

"Is there?" Carter glanced at the trees. Was there something large and hungry out there, watching them from a shadow?

"Have you been in the food business before? You kept calling the pub 'the establishment'."

"This is my first foray into restaurants." Carter smiled thinly. "I just wanted to use the right terminology; make sure everyone's clear."

"It makes things less clear," the wolf rejoined. "Calling it the Driftwood Pub would make it clear."

"Look," Carter said in an easy, open tone, ready to smooth feathers. "I can see you're not pleased with the idea of new ownership at the Driftwood. But I assure you, I want it to retain all of the rustic and authentic flavor that makes it so renowned. I'm not going to fire the owner—I want the expertise he offers as a local food guru. So really, all of this is only going to benefit James Falls as a whole."

The well-rehearsed words came naturally. Tell them everything would stay the same. Tell them their community would do well.

The wolf's face was unusually hard to read, though. He turned away to pick up the jug of coolant and opened the cap on the coolant reservoir.

"You're not going to buy the pub," he said, carefully pouring the blue-green liquid. "Why—"

Carter jumped in with a ready rebuttal. "Trust me, even though ownership is changing, the establishment will keep all of its small-town sparkle—"

The wolf had continued talking as well, and as a result Carter wasn't sure he heard correctly.

"I'm sorry?"

"I said, why do you think I cut your coolant line?" The wolf emptied the jug and replaced the reservoir cap, his eyes flicking up to Carter's face. "I wanted to have a talk, just you and me. It can be hard to get anything across with a pack of wolves looking over my shoulder."

In the following beat of silence, Carter gripped the hood to steady himself.

"Better check the engine temperature," the wolf said, striding quickly to the driver's seat. He flicked the car on, watching the dash.

Carter couldn't quite reconcile what he'd just heard with the wolf's manner. As the wolf stepped back out of the car, the lights flickering out again, nothing in his bearing suggested aggression or anger.

"It needs some time to cool. You've got a lot of mileage on this car for its age," the wolf remarked. "But I guess that makes sense, given that Driftwood Pub is three days' drive from here. South Bettony, right?"

Carter was again struck dumb. He stared at the wolf. How did he know about South Bettony? Last week, he and Bev had laid hold of a seaside eatery that drew people from miles around for its crab cakes…now that he heard it, Driftwood sounded right…

"I read about that one," the wolf went on. "You took the Driftwood over just recently. Left the owner as manager, and then you came here. But I get it, it's a recent acquisition. You might not be that familiar with the name of it yet."

Carter's mind raced. The wolf had baited him, used the wrong name on purpose. How could he have mixed up the names—how?!

The wolf broke his gaze, shutting the hood with a clap that nearly caused Carter to fall over. "The thing about wasting disease is," the wolf went on, leaning on the car, "while it's related to mad cow disease, there's never been a case where any effects were passed on by ingestion of the diseased meat. It's not transferable between species.

"That's supposing I saw an animal with the symptoms of wasting disease and still decided to sell it for people to eat." The wolf directed a pointed look at Carter. "I knew right away when that girl got sick. It wasn't the food." He waited. "Do you want to fill in the blanks for me?"

Carter attempted a laugh. "I'm not sure why you're telling me stories, but I need to get on the road."

"Then wait until I've reached the end," the wolf said. "So the sick girl. I asked myself, why would someone fake food poisoning, and why chalk it up to wasting disease? Why go to court over it? Why incur those costs?"

The wolf paused again, but Carter's mouth was too dry for him to form a reply, so he continued.

"It turns out, in the last few months there have been about six similar occurrences across the country. Remote places known for good food. They're up-and-coming sensations until they have a contamination scare, and then they have to be investigated. Every case I found went to court, and in every case nothing was proven—only that small restaurants can't afford city lawyers."

"I don't see what significance any of this holds for me," Carter spat. "If you'll excuse me." He strode past the wolf, half-expecting him to give chase, and opened the driver's side door.

His pocket buzzed, and Carter paused automatically, swiping the phone out of his pocket to see Bev's name on the caller screen.

It happened before he could react. The wolf pulled the phone out of his grasp and held it to his ear.

"This is Carter, how can I help you?" he said in a passable imitation of Carter's voice.

Carter was in shock. He made no movement as Bev's voice came through, loud enough for him to hear every word.

"Are you done *yet*? We need to close this one and skip for a few days, I think."

"How's the mad cow?" the wolf asked.

Her reply was so shrill there was no missing it. "Go to hell. Better yet, get them to sign and *then* go to hell. You got that? Hurry up, I've ordered Chinese."

She hung up, and the wolf pocketed Carter's phone. He resumed as though there had been no interruption.

"I've read six different articles about this kind of takeover, leaving the existing staff and ownership intact. It's a different holding company every time. But you know what's unusually similar?"

Carter had no idea. He was seriously thinking about diving into the car and running the wolf over.

"The quotes from the buyers. 'Small-town sparkle'. 'Keeping dollars in local pockets'. 'Local food gurus.' Isn't that strange?"

"Why do you care, anyway?" Carter snarled. The driver's door between them bolstered his courage. "You don't even live in James Falls! Them with their superstitions and their winter wolf!"

The wolf opened his jacket and dragged a giant folder, with difficulty, out of his inside pocket. Unfolding it, he waved it at Carter. It was the buyer's agreement he'd left with Adel.

"That, yeah. Winter wolf. They've been calling me that since I moved up the mountain. I put my winter supply trip off until the first snow, so things last longer. Yeah, they all have a good laugh...—but my name's Adel." He flipped through the pages of the agreement and showed Carter the last page, where a blank line waited beside the second owner's signature, denoted *W. Adel*.

Carter gulped for air, his mind spinning. "You-you're-you're the other Adel?"

The wolf nodded. "Do you remember what I told you about those crates?" he asked, nodding at the one sitting beside his truck. Carter's eye lurched there unwillingly.

With sudden, unthinking panic, Carter's body moved of its own accord. He sank into the car, slamming the door—

No keys. The keys were missing.

Leaning down outside his window, the wolf dangled them. They clattered against the glass. Carter's car keys.

Suddenly, the wolf looked skyward, distracted. "Look at that. I told you the snow was coming."

Carter could barely register it. Big, fluffy white flecks meandered down through the air, glowing brilliantly in the beams from the pickup's headlights.

The wolf opened the car door—Carter slammed it shut again, hitting the lock button—but the wolf unlocked it with the key fob and opened it again. He stood inside the door, squatting down, his yellow eyes flashing luridly in the headlights of the truck.

"Two options, Mr. Carter."

Nothing within Carter's reach would make an effective weapon. He didn't trust his strength anyway. He'd never needed it much.

"I've met a few of you city-born mutts, so I'm keeping it simple. Your first option is this: the money you would've used to purchase my pub—the *Knothole Pub*, if you're still confused—you will gift to us as a charitable donation, and then disappear forever from my town and my pack."

A silence stretched, softer and heavier as the scattering of snowflakes thickened into a flickering cascade of white, obscuring the trees, blurring the road...

Carter knew the wolf was waiting, and he resisted at first—but the wolf waited on with a patience that made no flutterings or misgivings, and Carter felt they might sit until the snow buried them.

"And option two?" he finally hissed, teeth gritted.

"You must read the news." The wolf smiled. "I told you I've met a few of you."

LONE
John Kulp

John Kulp is a rare, long-tailed, short-eared river wolf living in the inner harbor of Baltimore, MD, despite the best efforts of the coast guard. He enjoys sushi and pretty much any other form of fish, like any God-fearing wolf does. His hobbies include playing the board game go, table top gaming (always as a wolf, of course), and imbibing impossible quantities of tea, although he probably drinks meat water instead of leaf water because that sounds like what wolves would drink, but he certainly knows this because he is a wolf. You can follow him on twitter at @runningotter.

Randall Shepherd always felt most alone when he sat on the train. Often he found himself a shadowed, uncomfortable corner near the emergency exits to hide away. The illusion of closeness brought about by sitting next to someone else was inexplicably worse than just reveling in his own isolation. During the going-home bustle of Friday evenings, however, the only few open seats were always between other people.

The wolf's paws locked together tight on his lap. He stared at the long individual gray furs, blades of dying ashen grass over unkempt hills.

He tried to squeeze himself smaller. The ram on his right was too close. Wool pressed against the taut fabric over Randall's upper arm, and he prayed that his suit coat wasn't going to smell like lanolin until he could afford to have it washed. Sheep never got the hint when they invaded your personal space. If a blade of grass brushed over the tip of a single of the wolf's ankle furs, he'd notice immediately. Randall would have bet a paycheck on being able to scissor half a sheep's wool off before it realized.

A heaving sigh rustled the fur over his chest and neck, hand-trimmed short to keep the two sizes too small suit coat from bulging with the otherwise unkempt tufts. He wished for someone he could make that bet with. It wasn't that he wanted the money. Randall had no confidence that he could actually pull off a sheep shearing mid train ride. Even so, he liked to imagine the words he'd use, the way his voice would rise and fall, and the smirk on the shapeless muzzle of the figure he was talking to as he or she weighed the money versus getting to see the wolf try something so crazy.

He used to have friends back in high school and college. His old pack exchanged messages every once in a while, checking up on each other's lives and subtly boasting about their own. Everyone had married, fostered kids, and weren't all that interested in the nothings of the life of a lonely single accountant. They'd all wandered away to make new packs where there wasn't any room for Randall.

The wool rustled against his arm and shoulder, and then it was gone.

"Sorry," the ram said with an apologetic smile, "dozed off and didn't realize I got all up on you like that."

It felt like a blanket had been pulled away. Randall shivered.

When he got back to his apartment, he slammed the door. The wolf didn't know why. Nonsensical thoughts and emotions flooded his head, and his chest clenched like it was caught in a winch.

Randall paced back and forth the five steps he could manage in the tiny city apartment. He wanted to run. He wanted to scream. He panted short and ragged.

Is this what a heart attack felt like? A surge of panic threw him stumbling for his phone, buried in his pocket under an ocean of receipts, candy wrappers, and loose cigarettes. He tore it out and flipped it open, littering all the excess over his stained carpet. Shaking pads pressed nine one one.

He held still for a moment and steadied his breathing. No, this wasn't a heart attack. His head was clear. Nothing was spinning. He slowly slid the phone back into his pocket.

"Fuck," he said. Not bothering to take off his tightly hugging suit, the wolf collapsed onto his bed. At least his mom wasn't around to see him like this. She would have been worried sick for his wellbeing. The burly wolf woman always told him not to leave the farm, that the farm would keep him strong and healthy more than any dirty, gasoline- and tar-smelling city.

And Mom was dead, Dad was dead, the farm belonged to a brother whose birthday he didn't even remember, and he hadn't spoken to any of them in years.

Maybe she was right. College had been a shit idea.

The feeling returned, a deep burning in his chest. The fire bubbled and boiled inside him while his head swam with fear and pain and longing and want.

He got up from his bed. It was impossible to keep lying down while it felt like hot coals were going to burn right through him. Through instinct or feverish loss of control, the apartment window unlatched to his fumbling paws. It rose and let in the chilly exhaust-scented night air alongside the growls, screeches, and rumbles of the busy road seven stories below. He looked out and up at the faint stars and the sliver of a moon hanging low in the sky.

The tip of Randall's muzzle curled into an O, and he let loose a howl that echoed despair through the city streets and skyscrapers. His vocal cords strained and cracked, but he pushed through with the song. It felt so right. All the pent-up emotion, the loneliness and banality of life, poured out of his lungs and into the gentle breeze. He held the note as long as he could, a sharp, piercing tenor spear through the droll white noise of city life.

Was this what vacuous wolves felt like when they howled with their packs? Did they sing just like him to release the pain and anxieties of life? Or was there more to it; a pack closeness bound in blood and shrill notes to the heavens?

That closeness was a puzzle piece for the empty spot in Randall's heart.

He hadn't howled since he was a young cub on the farm. His mom scolded him, dragged him inside by the ear, and sternly said that no *civilized* wolf would ever be seen howling like that. Afterward, he held off for eighteen years.

Why would canines restrain themselves when howling felt so good?

But his was the only note cutting through the sky.

Someone yelled from a window above to shut the fuck up. Randall sheepishly ducked his head back in and slid it closed. His paw hung over the latch, ready to lock it again, but he didn't. He liked the wildness that had rushed through his body and sent shivers across his fur. He couldn't bear losing that last meager connection. Another howl would be far too embarrassing, but he relished the idea that he could. The window was unlocked if he needed to throw it open and sing to the night sky again.

The next day, a notice taped to his door said that he owed the landlord two hundred dollars in restitution for the public disturbance the previous night. A postscript politely informed him that if he were to ever try that again, it was well within the landlord's rights to evict him.

After an initial bout of anxiety, he crumpled the notice and stuffed it deep into the pocket of his dress pants. As he walked to the train station, he began to mentally plan which meals he was going to have to skip to pay the fee. Maybe his suit would almost fit, then. A grin formed on his muzzle, but then evaporated when he realized he wanted to tell someone else and for them to laugh right along with him.

Randall didn't hate his boss, but it wasn't a close camaraderie either. Of course, he doubted anyone had that kind of relationship with the sharply dressed mouse. Stereotypes be damned, Randall was less scared walking alone at night through the government-assisted housing blocks near his apartment than he was getting called in to talk to Timothy.

"Sir," he started. The mouse didn't even look up from his computer. "Sir?"

"Yes, yes! Continue! What is it that you wish to ask?" The mouse's nasally voice sliced through Randall's nerves like a cheese knife against a wheel of camembert.

"I was wondering—excuse me, I was hoping that if it were possible I could maybe get an advance. Well, you know…" Randall trailed off.

"No, I do not know. What sort of *advance* do you need, and why exactly do you need it?"

"I, well, I need two hundred dollars. I got a noise disturbance notice and—"

"And you wish for me to save your tail after you host one of those wild parties all you pups hold? If I were to cover for every inane decision made by an employee of mine, I would add hours to my salary calculations, potentially costing the company money that would no longer be present for allocation to bonuses or raises. Next time, think about the consequences before you choose to hold a shindig during sleeping hours."

"But I—"

"That is all. Please return to your work."

Randall left the office with his tail between his legs. Had Timothy even looked up from his computer while he was talking? Randall couldn't remember.

The first half hour of overtime was spent filling out an overtime request form. Another two went by filling out tax forms that weren't due for another month as he hoped that his boss would find it somewhere in his mechanical mouse heart to approve retroactive overtime as well.

By the time he started for home, dusk had already blanketed the city. At least the train was nearly empty. Time felt slower, dragging out his commute to feel twice as long as usual.

However, when Randall laid down on his soft bed in his closed-off apartment, he finally felt like he could relax. He was alone but warm, with faux fur covers around his shoulders that made him feel like someone else was cuddled up close to him.

He turned on the television to drown out his mind. Most of the news hour flew straight over his head. It never seemed to stick after long days staring at numbers on a computer. However, his ears perked the end of the program.

"That's right. We regret to inform you that Yule, the last known vacuous grey wolf, has passed away in captivity. It is a tragedy for sure, but we can rest easy knowing that he is joining his mate Yuna, who succumbed to a fever last month.

"Scientists have been on the search for any signs of vacuous grey wolves out in the wild, but their findings are grim. Since our last report on Yuna, many of our viewers have written in with their own accountings of wolf sightings or instances of howlings. However, our follow-up investigations indicate that all could be accounted for, most originating around sapient canines. Still, we appreciate your help in an attempt to prove wrong this tragic news. A source informs me that the extinction will likely be announced within the year.

"After Yuna's passing, Yule was devastated. He paced his enclosure for her, circling the location out on the grass where her body had been extracted. He howled more in that month than he had in his lifetime before. Although I view this tragedy with a heavy heart, I don't believe that we sapient peoples, no matter the species, can find a better example of undiluted companionship than between these two vacuous wolves."

The wolf hit the power on the remote, and his apartment drowned in silence.

Randall decided that he needed a pack. He needed a Yuna for his Yule. He needed to be a wolf.

For the first of his two hours of still-unapproved overtime the next day, he searched the internet for local wolf associations. The nearest one met on Thursdays at a bar by the docks, but all the pictures posted on their web page featured burly beasts of wolves, the kinds that used to play bikers in action movies. Even if they howled together and hung out as a close pack, he didn't think that he'd fit in.

Randall moved on to hobby groups. However, he had no hobbies. Back in college he spent a lot of time getting really good at Rubik's cubes, but that wasn't something that he could do with other people. Instead he browsed the listings in the area, looking for something that didn't seem too difficult or intimidating. The crochet club was perfect.

They met every week after work at six o'clock on Friday. Even better, the club met only a few blocks from the towering office building where he worked, in the second floor of an unassuming wooden coffee shop nestled snug between two glass and aluminum Goliaths.

He stopped by the coffee shop during lunchtime that Thursday so that he could get a feel for the place. It was important to be comfortable with the building before throwing himself into the terrifying situation of confronting the group and asking to join.

On Friday, he brought in a bag full of bathroom supplies to trim his fur, smooth his suit jacket, and beautify his scent after work in order to be as fresh and presentable as he could manage. After prettying up and stashing the bag in his desk drawer, he briskly walked to the coffee shop with much more confidence than he believed that he warranted.

However, his confidence evaporated like a puddle on a sunny July sidewalk when he stepped inside. The rabbit girl at the counter smiled at him wide, bright, and buck-toothed.

Randall approached her and asked in a hushed mutter, as if he were protecting a critical secret, "Is the crochet club upstairs?"

"That's right! They should be starting in a few minutes. Stairs are through that door and it's the room on the left!"

The wolf nodded a quick thanks, took a few steps, and then realized that it was probably impolite not to order something. Flustered, he turned back and paid for a jasmine tea which the rabbit prepared without even momentarily breaking her sunny smile. He ascended the narrow stairway cup in paw, steadied himself, and then opened the door.

The crochet club consisted of a bunch of women sitting in a circle in a sparse wooden room. Tables had been shoved out to the edges, where several non-matching wardrobes and dressers were stacked with haphazard clusters of yarn and board games. Even though there was certainly enough space, the roof, so steep that it nearly touched the back of the chair nearest the far wall, instilled a mild claustrophobia in Randall.

"Don't just stand there! Come right on in!" a sheep lady laughed. His ears and muzzle flushed with heat, but he quickly shut the door behind him and stepped forward several paces before realizing that he didn't know which of the several empty seats in the circle of chairs would be right to take. He didn't want to accidentally steal someone else's seat only to have them come in moments later to kick him out. "You're here for crochet?" she continued. A waggle of ears and tails around the room choreographed the members' surprise.

Randall winced. "Yeah."

At that, everyone started to talk. Voices fought and clambered over one another to rise to the top, but none managed to do so. The wolf's tail drooped, and his ears flattened.

"Shush! One at a time!" A deer on the far side of the chair circle raised her hand. Everyone quieted down. Tails and ears hung low in embarrassment. Randall mentally marked her as the alpha.

"You can sit next to me if you'd like," she happily offered. Randall nodded and sat himself in the seat she gestured to.

After they got settled and the deer, whose name he learned was Sarah, guided his unsteady paws through a basic stitch, the room slowly buzzed back to life with conversation. At first he didn't pay attention. Mistakenly, the focus of his attention was on the crochet. Crochet club, he quickly realized, wasn't actually about crochet. It was about having an excuse to gossip with friends every week.

A brown bear halfway around the circle from Randall talked about how her boyfriend hadn't been returning her calls at night. Karen, an outspoken hyena, told her that she should just drop him. The relationship was over; he wasn't in it anymore. He'd never really been there for her anyway. It had always just been about him and what he wanted.

The wolf smiled and followed along as best he could without knowing the tangled, interconnected web of relationships serving as a background for each story. The women seemed to know everything about each other's lives; which sibling was causing strife with the family, their favorite music to work to, or even how they liked their toast and eggs in the mornings.

"What about you—Randall, right? That's what you said your name was?" Karen asked.

He nodded.

"What's happening in the life of this handsome, stately wolf?"

"Oh shut it, Karen! If he wants to talk, he'll talk." The edges of Sarah's long deer muzzle curled.

"It's no problem," Randall said. "Really, it's fine. I don't think it'll be as interesting as any of your stories, though."

Sarah was suddenly smiling again. Leaving her crochet needles and half-knitted hoof-toed socks on her lap, she set a hand on Randall's paw. "Don't say that! Everyone's got an interesting story or two in them. Hey, why don't you tell us what brought you here?"

The wolf's ears and muzzle flushed with heat, but he nodded despite himself. Sarah hadn't taken her hand away. An almost imperceptible blush darkened the skin under the hood of her flicking conical deer ears as well. "It was a news story actually, two nights ago on channel 7. They were talking about Yule, he was, you know—"

"The last vacuous wolf! That was so sad!" Lydia, a fluffed-up and well-pampered arctic fox, interjected.

The deer's shush held enough venom to kill a small animal. "He's new! Let him talk! I'm sorry about that. Go on then, as you were saying."

He hesitantly told them that there was a little of himself that he saw in the vacuous wolves, that he'd been stuck in his stale life for too long. Especially after the little bit of release he'd gotten on Tuesday.

"What happened on Tuesday? Did you—did you *meet* someone?" This time, it was all Sarah doing the poking and prodding. Everyone else was either amusedly watching on as they crocheted colorful designs in their laps or laughing to each other in hushed conversations.

He shook his head, wanting to crawl deep inside himself where he wouldn't have to admit to anyone. "I howled." Several women snickered, but Sarah swept the room with a glare that could shrivel an elephant. "I couldn't help it. There was all this pressure welling up inside of me like a steam vent, and I had to turn the valve and let it loose somehow. And you know—you know what, it felt really damn good."

At some point when he was talking, the rusted padlock on the safe of feelings and emotions he'd held hidden deep inside him clattered to the floor. He opened up like a bottle of champagne. Over the next hour, he told them about everything from his lonesome howl out the window of his apartment to the isolation of his train rides. Sarah's soft, brown-furred hand never left his.

It felt really good to confide in the women of the crochet club. Despite the snickers when he started, everyone took him seriously. They listened and nodded along and interjected occasionally with questions or bits of helpful advice.

"Look, you need to actually talk to your boss. He didn't hear the story, and he'd understand if you told him how it really went down," the arctic fox suggested.

"But he wouldn't understand! He's like a robot in mouse fur! He doesn't care what my problem is, just what cents it would cost the multi-million dollar fucking conglomerate!"

"You're just going to go up to him and say—"

"Hey Tim," Randall said, glancing nervously over the bulky CRT monitor on Tim's desk, "I wasn't able to give you the full story when I was telling you what happened. Would you please give me a moment to explain myself?"

"You may. Go ahead."

Randall did his very best not to shake as he looked down at the furiously typing mouse. "I may have—I mean, I did something stupid, but it wasn't a party. I just had this embarrassing moment where everything was too much, and I accidentally howled. It sort of just happened."

The mouse didn't interject like last time, so Randall continued. "But anyway, I've been working for you for three years now. I've always done my job and met my deadlines, and I've never asked for something like this before. Would you please reconsider giving me an advance on my next paycheck? I promise that it won't happen again."

There were a few seconds of silence before Timothy said, "Are you finished speaking?"

Randall shivered. "Yeah."

"Very well. You may have the advance. We are friends, are we not?"

"What?"

The mouse stopped typing and looked up from his computer with a slight tilt of his head. "Did I misread that? Are we not friends? But we had beers three months ago for a Friday happy hour. I considered that to be an indication of friendship."

"No!" Randall interjected. "We're friends! Yeah, we're friends, you were right."

"Oh, good."

"Hey," the wolf said, ears flipping nervously, "how would you like to get drinks again next Thursday?"

"Would Friday not be more suitable? A hangover would severely impact our productivity."

"I've got something on Fridays now."

"Oh. Good for you. Thursday would be nice."

Randall walked into the crochet club with a triumphant smile stretching his muzzle in a way that he hoped wasn't intimidating. The women, only a fifth of them there a quarter hour early, greeted him with welcoming enthusiasm.

When Sarah came in and sat next to him, he excitedly recounted the talk he had with his boss. She smiled wide, congratulated him, and then offered a hug which the wolf, after a moment of sheepish doubt, accepted.

The second week was easier and more familiar than the first. With friends to talk to and the sudden problem of where the two hundred dollar fine would come from solved, he felt much lighter. He happily gossiped along with the group, throwing anecdotes of his own life in to mesh with their stories and problems. A surge of pride bubbled a glowing warmth under his fur the first time Karen, the hyena, nodded and said that what he'd suggested sounded like good advice.

The drudging banality of daily life began to quicken as Randall found his mind always occupied with the stories he was going to tell his new friends and the look on Sarah's stubby, speckled muzzle when he chose to speak up. After a month, he realized that he wasn't even conscientious about where to sit on the train anymore.

As spring blossomed into summer, Randall felt like he was a new wolf.

When he walked into the coffee shop, early as usual, the women were all sitting around downstairs. His first instinct was dread. It wasn't normal for everyone to show up as early as him, and certainly not for them to wait down on the first floor. He was about to ask if something was wrong when Laura, a tomboyish bobcat, noticed him. "Hey, Randall's here!"

Sarah hopped right out of her seat, and everyone else followed more leisurely. "Randall!" she exclaimed. "You're here! Hey, so I was thinking that we'd do something different today. I was talking with the girls, and we decided to, well, I don't want to ruin the surprise. Come on, follow me!"

She led the group several blocks to the east where the city bustled with more commercial blocks. Instead of the homogeneous office buildings and the coffee shops and sandwich shops crowding first floors, neon signs hung glowing off the edges of massive malls and shopping centers, advertising everything from groceries to hobby shops to craft stores.

It had been years since Randall last scraped up a valid reason to surround himself with the roiling sea of after-work shoppers perusing the extravagant displays on the stores wealthy enough to afford a space on the ground floor. He used to find it oppressive with the musks of every species imaginable, foreign and local, fighting with the foul stench of sun on pavement for control of his nostrils.

But it wasn't as bad when he could laugh with his friends about how terribly gaudy the dresses in the windows were. Karen said that the more she walked though there, the more she was sure that they were marketing to lottery-winning hookers. A scowl from the arctic fox corrected her to "working girls."

They ended up on a backstreet several corners down from the main throughway. Sarah stopped and gestured down a flight of stairs leading into the basement of a squat building, half the size of the gigantic shopping centers they'd been looking at before. The sign above glowed "53rd street Karaoke" in fluorescent ruby letters.

"Karaoke?" Randall asked, confused.

"Don't knock it 'till you try it," she said with her usual confidence.

Sarah paid the receptionist for two hours in a large enough room to fit the entire club. Randall protested when he saw how fat the bill was, but the deer just shushed him and said that this was what club dues were for.

The room was long and thin with no more space than was necessary to fit the cushioned wall-mounted seating and the table that was just wide enough to be slightly uncomfortable for everyone, thick or thin. Randall ended up along the back wall, smushed between Sarah and Karen.

"So, who's gonna start?" Randall said with a nervous chuckle after everyone was seated. They knew him well enough to know he wouldn't want to, but his nerves suggest they'd volunteer him anyway.

Much to his relief, Sarah said, "I will." However, she didn't grab for the little tablet-like console that controlled the karaoke machine. Instead, the doe's muzzle pointed up at the ceiling and she cried out "Awoooo!"

Her shout didn't sound like a real howl. It didn't have the right pitch or the same piercing edge as a canine's. However, Randall understood. The doe's paw slid over his and squeezed as her faux howl hung in the stuffy air of the small room.

His stomach twisted, and his throat clenched. Tears threatened the wolf's eyes making him blink furiously, trying and failing to fight them back. He buried his muzzle in the crook of his arm.

Karen reached around him to rustle Sarah's shoulder. The room fell back into silence.

"Hey, are you okay?" Sarah asked after a hesitant pause.

"Yeah," Randall choked back. No one said anything for the next minute, so he forced himself to continue. "Thank you so much. You—you all have no idea how much this means to me." He trembled.

His stomach turned on itself, and pressure tightened his chest and lungs. For a moment, he wondered if he was going to throw up, praying that he wouldn't embarrass himself that badly. However, after a moment, he realized what his body wanted from him.

As he raised his head from his paws, the women in the room looked at him with a mix of expectation and unease. He tilted his muzzle toward the ceiling, and released the clear sharp note of his howl.

One by one, the women of the crochet club joined in on the chorus, only the yippy arctic fox even canine. The floodgates behind wolf's eyes couldn't be stopped up. Amid the playful shouts and encouraging cries of "Awoo! Awoooo!" the crisp song of the wolf echoed in the small, soundproof karaoke room.

None of his new friends understood the language of the howl. They couldn't comprehend how the subtleties of the shifts in his pitch wove his story of discovery and acceptance. However, they understood the expression on his face as he sang out to the moon that he couldn't see through brick and plaster. They knew the meaning behind the tears that matted the fur under his eyes.

As his song faded back to nothingness, Sarah's soft hand pulled his muzzle back down to her level and the lips of the Yuna to his Yule locked passionately with his own.

STEALING THE SHOW
Jaden Drackus

Jaden Drackus, or Jay Dee is not a wolf, though he does play one in video games. Rather, he is a foxdragon from Maryland (so 1/8th wolf, once removed, maybe?). Born in 1983, he has been writing furry stories since officially stumbling into the fandom in 2010. Since then he has written in his spare time to remain sane while pursuing his bachelor's in military history, which he achieved in 2016.

A video gamer, builder of model airplanes, reader, and keen observer of Life's little ironies Jay Dee lives in Baltimore with a pack that consists of his boyfriend and 4 cats.

His work can be found at http://www.furaffinity.net/user/jaden drackus/. His silly observations on life and occasional attempts to start howls can be seen on Twitter: @JadenDrakus.

"You ready?" the voice asked in the darkness behind the entryway, interrupting my meditations.

I opened my eyes and looked at the owner of that voice, a large cougar in a suit who went by the stage name of Duce: my boss in the Global Champions Wrestling League, GCW for short. Most cougars are bigger than wolves like me, and Duce was huge even for a cougar, so I had to look up to meet his gaze. I could see his eyes glowing in the darkness, like most cats. I considered him for a moment and realized the question was half genuine concern, half challenge. Fortunately, I was up for a challenge. My ears flicked, and I looked at the other person standing in the entrance to the stage before responding.

"Yeah, we're ready," I replied confidently, though I had to admit I was a bit nervous. It was GCW's last televised show before their big fall pay-per-view, and I had been given a big task to perform that night—one that could make or break my career. The second wrestler in the entryway nodded their confirmation as I responded to Duce.

I don't know if Duce could smell my nervousness, since feline noses aren't as sensitive as canine ones, but I sure could. It filled the air back stage before I popped the scent-reducing gel cover on my nose. I could tell my dance partner was nervous too, but they were also hiding it. The big cougar clapped me on the shoulder and looked both me and the other person in the eyes before playfully shoving me toward the curtain that separated us from the rest of the arena.

"Steal my show," he whispered in my ear as he pushed me.

Any reply I could make was drowned out by the opening guitar chord of my rock-themed entrance music. I took a deep breath and stepped out into the odd world of professional wrestling. The oddity of the world was driven home as soon as I stepped out on the stage: I smiled as the crowd booed at me. What other world would boos be the desired reaction? I stood on the stage for a moment, staring at the floor, the black lights heralding my entrance and igniting the designs airbrushed into my fur to an eerie moonlike glow. A moment later, I threw my head back and let out a long howl that probably caused a lot of ears to go flat in the audience. The boos continued, although they were broken up here and there with the occasional cheer as the lights came up and exposed me to any in the crowd that didn't have good night vision. I bared my fangs and growled briefly before I set off at an unhurried pace down the ramp to the ring.

Professional wrestling is a strange beast, and a lot of people get turned off by the fact that it shares a name with an Olympic sport. So they decry it as fake because the outcomes of the matches are predetermined. I prefer to compare it to gladiatorial combat in Ancient Rome—with the wrinkle that before every battle the Emperor said something like "I really want to see that tiger with the net and trident win." So you went out and had the fight so that the tiger won, because it was the Emperor, and he was paying for all of this. The result is something akin to full-contact thespianism: you had to have the skills of both an athlete and an actor.

I was about halfway to the ring when the announcer shouted my performing name of Mark Lycos to the crowd. Not very original, I know, since it's just the Greek word for "wolf," but if you're familiar with professional wrestling you know wolves are very rare in the business. I was the only one of my species in GCW on that night; there was a pair working as a tag team in developmental, since creative usually stuck with the "pack" stereotype role when wolves do appear in the business. In the old days, wolves were pack hunters—team players, and in the past there had been some pretty famous wolf pack tag teams. Not me though, I was a lone wolf, and GCW played that for all it was worth. I puffed my chest to display my official t-shirt, which proclaimed that I was "All Alpha;" and that I had "No Pack, No Fear."

That's all nonsense, of course. The "lone wolf" and "alpha wolf" are myths and movie tropes cooked up by other species that don't really get us wolves. Maybe it was cougars like Duce, who have a history of being loners that came up with it. I have a pack (what most other species would call a family). In fact, my phone back in my bag in the locker room was probably filling up with pictures of our newest member, my brother's cub. The pack is everything to us, even if we sometimes play act otherwise.

I hopped up on to the apron of the ring before climbing the turnbuckle to my right, and flexed for the crowd. I didn't really see them; I don't pay a lot of attention to how many people are in the crowd—it helps keep me from getting stage fright. I could hear them just fine though; it's hard not to hear with these big pointed ears of mine. Their reaction was mixed: mostly boos, but more than a few cheers as well. The boos are expected since I'm a heel, the wrestling term for a bad guy, and the cheers are a sign of respect for my performance. I've been wrestling for many years on the independent circuit and in Japan, so I'd built up a bit of a following. Tonight, I heard those cheers a little louder, and strutted a little more. Tonight, I needed the assurance that I would put on a good show and be appreciated, despite being the bad guy. I hopped down, crossed the ring to the opposite turnbuckle, and posed to the crowd on that side. I licked my nose to hide a smile—it was good to be around a lot of people; people are always interesting.

I am fairly large for a wolf: both in height, at a bit over six foot two at the tip of my ears, and in mass, as I had 245 pounds of pure muscle packed under my dark gray and white fur. Well, it had been white, I dyed my white fur a dark red to go with my bad guy persona. Blood red, the commentators liked to claim. I kept it closely trimmed to show off my physique, though at the moment it was obscured by that tight fitting tee shirt. I hopped down off the turnbuckle and strutted to the side of the ring with the commentators' tables. The badger ring announcer held out a microphone between the ropes, and I snatched it from his paw. I took a deep breath and settled fully in to my heel personality as I inhaled the crowd's scent. Not a bad crowd tonight, at least as much as I could smell through the gel cap on my nose. There was the typical US mix of species smells: canines, mustelids, cervines, bovines, equines, and felines— all of various ages. Thankfully for my nose, there were not many that were scent neutralizer adverse, nor many that thought drowning themselves in it was a replacement for bathing. I took one more breath, and brought the mic up to my muzzle: it was time to exercise the acting half of being a professional wrestler. I let my hackles raise, my teeth show, and my legs and tail go stiff in the typical way we wolves show dominance.

"I don't think I need to remind any of you that Fall Brawl is this Sunday," I growled into the mic as I prowled around the ring. A few cheers for the mention of the event. "And in what is clearly a mistake, I—one of the best damn wrestlers in this business— don't have a match on the card."

That was my heel act: a cocky, arrogant, rather self-absorbed wrestler who had made his name on the independent circuit and came to GCW to prove that he was among the best in the world. I didn't need anyone's help: I was a lone wolf, and I could climb the ladder on my own talents, even though the idea was nonsense outside the story GCW was telling. I let the boos that my comment inspired continue without any further remark. I had made the decision early on that though I would be annoyed with the crowd for not recognizing my greatness, I wouldn't verbally attack them like some other heels did. In the eyes of some, that fact made it okay to cheer me. Duce liked it, because it meant that he wouldn't have a job on his hands if he wanted to turn me babyface—a good guy.

"And you wanna know why I don't have a match this Sunday?" I asked the crowd with a snarl. "It's because there ain't nobody in the GCW who can take me pound for pound. No—"

I was cut off by the start of a strange to the crowd Eastern-influenced entrance song. The lights in the arena went out, leaving everything in darkness except for the images flickering on the jumbo screen above the entrance. A moment later, the music hit a crescendo, and the lights rose to reveal the orange, cream, and black fur of the most handsome red fox ever. He was dressed in green leather pants and a matching vest covered in silver disks that sparkled as his breathing moved them. His head hung down, his eyes closed, but after a moment they opened, and he challenged me with that beautiful shit-eating grin that all foxes do so well. I frowned to hide my own smirk as a small but vocal portion of the crowd erupted into cheers.

Tetsukitsune the Iron Fox, one of the biggest wrestling sensations of Japan, had arrived in GCW. Tetsu's eyes came up and met mine as he all but danced down the ramp to the ring. It was clear from his gaze that Tetsu was partly thinking about what would happen in our hotel room later that night.

Yeah. We're lovers. A gay couple in the locker room isn't as odd a concept as most people would assume in a macho industry like wrestling. Not that I broadcasted it any more than was absolutely necessary. I preferred to keep my personal life, well, personal and the guys in the locker room respected that. They'd learned that I was pro-LBGT, as I would sometimes chide them for using homophobic language the way you would chide someone for swearing. They accepted it as "Mark's thing" and let it go. That was how these things went.

Tetsu and I had met while we were both wrestling in Japan. Now eight years later I had suggested that GCW bring him in, which meant I had to tell Duce about us. Surprisingly, the cougar thought it was a good thing. He said it took out one of the major booking headaches, the clash of egos. Because we were a couple, neither of us would try to make ourselves look better at the other's expense. Both of us would want the other to look as good as possible.

Tetsu was part of my pack, so I'd make him look good anyway— though the nuance of that would probably be lost on the cougar. The fox, for his part, found the idea of being in a wolf pack hilarious. But Duce had ultimately left it in my paws to make it work. It was up to me to make the crowd understand why the Iron Fox was special. It was up to me to make them cheer Tetsu. If we succeeded in getting Tetsu over with the crowd, the possibilities were almost endless. If we failed…it would be back to relative obscurity and lower paying matches—for both of us. The nerves I'd felt back stage returned full force, and I forced my tail to remain still. My ears remained in motion, trying to get a read from the crowd. If Tetsu was feeling anything similar, his tail and ears didn't show it, as they seemed to be moving in time with his music.

Tetsu entered the ring, and we circled each other until he wound up on the announcer side and secured a mic of his own. His scent penetrated my nose cover: woody, tinged with the pine and citrus of the scent powder I bought him last month. He was probably wearing it deliberately, and the gesture eased a few of the butterflies I was feeling. I put my own mic back up to my muzzle while Tetsu waved up at the section of crowd that was chanting his name. My tail twitched in what I hoped was a good imitation of agitation. His was a relaxed arc behind him. I went stiff again, raising my hackles even more as I tried to make myself bigger than he was. Not difficult: Tetsu was a good five inches shorter than me, and was about forty pounds lighter. That made my trying to assert my dominance look petty to any wolves in the audience, and possibly scary to other species. I'd had to apologize back stage to a few of the smaller guys that didn't know that such displays were just how wolves communicate, and not actual threats. Tetsu was having none of it—he knew me better than anyone.

"What the hell are you doing here, *teki*?" I asked with my teeth bared, using the word that Tetsu had taught me for "rival."

"Oh, not much," Tetsu replied in excellent English that often surprised crowds unfamiliar with him. He'd actually been born in New York, and moved to Japan when he was eight. "I came here because of you, *ani*." That meant "brother," and Tetsu used it both in the mock affection of our rivalry in the ring and in the genuine affection of our real life relationship.

I frowned, focusing on keeping up my dominant appearance (ears forward, tail and legs stiff, teeth slightly bared) as I faced him. His tail continued moving in slow sedate arcs behind him. He raised a paw and pointed at me lazily.

"I've been watching you *ani*," he continued, ignoring my displays of dominance with the lack of concern only a fox could manage. "You go on and on about how you've come to GCW to prove you are the best in the world."

"I am the best," I growled back at him. "You should know that by now. More than anyone."

He smiled, and I frowned a little harder so that I wouldn't return it. We could both hear it: there was a buzz in the crowd, not a loud one but it was there. Enough of them had seen our matches in Japan to have some idea what to expect, and the rest had picked up on that excitement. It was time for us to earn that excitement. I flicked my left ear, the sign to Tetsu that we needed to get down to business. Tetsu flicked his own ear in acknowledgement.

"I am...unconvinced," the fox said. "I think the score is tied between us."

"Well *teki*, we can fix that right...now!" I snarled, tossing down the mic before pulling my shirt off. The fact that I had come to the ring in my wrestling trunks and knee pads to deliver a speech was just one of those odd things about wrestling you just have to accept. I pointed to the weasel in a striped referee shirt standing at ringside and jerked my thumb toward me to indicate he should get in the ring. Across from me, Tetsu smirked, his tail swishing just a bit faster than it had been.

"Oh *ani*. Perhaps you've already forgotten what it is like to deal with strong style."

That definitely popped the crowd. They had heard of that style and knew what it meant. Wrestling has a lot of different styles from grappling to striking to brawling, but strong style has gained a global interest since it came out of Japan about a decade ago. Strong style mixes in a lot of martial arts type moves into the traditional grapples and strikes in my more traditional move set. But the biggest thing about it from being on the wrong side of it: practitioners of strong style tend to hit for real rather than pulling their moves and trusting their opponent to act like they hurt more than they did, which was called selling in wrestling parlance. There had been more than a few nights after we had matches that Tetsu and I had shared ice tubs because we'd beaten the holy hell out of each other.

With a flick of his wrist, the fox tossed his microphone out of the ring before he whipped his vest off and threw it after the mic. Then we circled each other as I snarled, and Tetsu smiled at me.

"Watashi no aozora, itsu made mo," he whispered just before we locked our paws on each other's shoulders. He always said that before our matches: "I always love you." Although with my incomplete command of Japanese, I wasn't sure that's what he actually said. I did know he'd started saying that before our third match after we started dating: he'd cried into my shoulder after splitting my nose open in our second match. After that, he always made sure I knew that he wasn't really trying to hurt me.

"Un, wakaru," I growled. He'd told me it meant "I know." Again, I wasn't sure if it was completely correct, but all that mattered was that it was our little ritual. I knew that he would never intentionally hurt me, but if he felt better saying it, I was all for it.

I turned my attention to Tetsu, and my ears to the level of noise coming from the crowd. Right now it was a low buzz, broken here and there by clusters of cheers from fans who had either seen our previous encounters or liked my or Tetsu's style.

I had worked hard for those little clusters: in GCW, I was an anomaly. Technically, I was a heavyweight, but as a wolf, I was thought too small for a weight class dominated by bovines, equines, and big cats like Duce. The internet liked to claim that GCW's owner, a cougar named Victor O'Malley (who happened to be Duce's father-in-law), didn't like smaller guys like me. I don't know if that was true, but he did have a preference for the big guys—which meant that Tetsu and I had to earn our place. I growled to prevent a nervous whimper from escaping from my muzzle. Tetsu returned it with a mocking growl of his own.

Duce gave us six minutes to work with. If the former wrestler liked what he saw, and more importantly heard, we had a shot at bigger things. If not…I didn't want to think about that as I went into the first sequence of moves with Tetsu.

For those that are unfamiliar with wrestling, the goal of the affair is of course to defeat your opponent. In a traditional rules match, there are four ways to do this: first, pin their shoulders to the mat for three seconds as counted by the referee; second, get them to submit to an aptly named submission hold; third, make it so they cannot reenter the ring in ten seconds, again counted by the referee; or finally, by beating your opponent so brutally that they couldn't answer a ten count. So the goal of wrestling is to weaken your opponent to the point where one of those conditions is an option. Because professional wrestling is a performance art, wrestlers tend to have an arsenal of signature moves to get a pop from the crowd, and one that is designed to put their opponent away as a finishing move. For a social species like a wolf, there was nothing like hearing an arena full of people all reacting your show.

Tetsu and I began our dance. We slapped our paws on each other's shoulders and tried to shove each other backward. After a moment, Tetsu wiggled out and slid behind me trying for a choke hold, but I spun around, and we locked up again. I dropped to my knees and attempted to hook my arm through

Tetsu's own knee. The fox was ready for that, however, and moved with my motion, flipping and landing on his paws before lunging at me with a knee to my shoulder. I fell to my stomach on the mat, and Tetsu continued the assault, driving his knee into my ribs again and again. After four strikes, I managed to roll to the ropes, and the ref pulled Tetsu off me as I used the middle rope to pull myself to my paws. The crowd was buzzing a bit, since strikes like that weren't seen often in GCW, and they were taking notice: I even heard a few swears coming from the first couple rows. We had their attention, but we had to keep it. The ref tried to physically separate us, but Tetsu ignored him just long enough to kick me in the head. I leaned heavily against ropes before resuming my climb to my paws.

Meanwhile Tetsu bounced off the ropes on the other side of the ring and rebounded toward me. His plan didn't come through: I lunged forward, clotheslining him so hard that he flipped completely over and landed on his back. I knelt in the middle of the ring huffing and exposing my fangs while Tetsu writhed next to me. Meanwhile, the crowd roared in shock and approval. I pulled Tetsu to his paws as I whispered in his pointed ear my idea for the next sequence of moves. Tetsu grunted, the only sign of agreement.

I bent him over, grabbed hold of the waistband of his pants and lifted him over my head as I fell backward in a suplex, slamming Tetsu on his back. But the agile fox flipped around in mid-air, landed on his paws, and fired off a kick at me. I was ready, and swung my left arm up to block the fox's black foot paw before I slammed my elbow into the side of the fox's muzzle. The crowd was definitely getting into it as Tetsu staggered, and came back with an elbow of his own. I lurched back a step and shook my head. Tetsu had connected just enough to set my ears ringing. As I lashed back, I could feel my tail wagging ever so slightly in pride. Tetsu's was twitching as well.

The crowd popped as we traded four more pairs of elbows before Tetsu grabbed my neck and threw three rapid-fire blows before slamming a knee into my stomach. I doubled over, and Tetsu shoved my head under his arm and grabbed my trunks.

"*Itanderu made daisuki wa yo*" he murmured. He's never fully explained what that means and with my tourist level command of Japanese, I could only pick out "I love you," but he only whispers it before we do something that will really hurt. Then he suplexed me.

That impressed the crowd, since they clearly didn't quite believe that the shorter, leaner fox could lift a bulky wolf like me. Tetsu was on me in a heartbeat and tried locking in an arm bar submission hold. I countered by interlacing my fingers together so he couldn't get a full grip on my arm. We stayed that way for several moments, the smaller fox on top of me, his ruddy orange fur a vivid contrast to my dark red and gray fur. I kept growling and fluffing my fur out, trying to show that I wasn't in a tight spot—I was still the dominant one. But I also brought my tail up between my legs in a subtle give away that I wasn't so sure about that. As we struggled, the ref leaned down on the pretense of seeing if I wanted to submit. What he was really doing was relaying to us what he'd heard on his ear piece.

"Duce says go for top spot," he whispered.

Top spot, the code phrase that indicated that we had impressed the powers that be enough to earn the match at Fall Brawl. Our tails thrashed against each other's in our excitement as we snarled at each other, our noses touching as we prepared the finish we'd planned. Tetsu finally gave up trying to lock in the arm bar and settled for punching me in the chest before rolling to his paws. He hauled me up for another suplex, but I blocked it before slamming a knee into his stomach and pulling his head down under my arm. I glared out at the crowd, threw my head back, and howled. That popped the crowd again, as it was the sign that I was going for my finisher: a variation on the old DDT move that I called the Moonsetter. All I had to do was drop to my back and slam Tetsu's head to the canvas, and that would be it. But Tetsu had taken more than his fair share of Moonsetters and was ready for it.

He dropped a paw behind my knee and yanked, dropping me on my back before leaning over to shake a finger at me. This was followed by a vicious knee drop that actually did pinch my ears a bit, though I sold it like it had landed squarely on my forehead. I writhed around while Tetsu slowly stood up. He dragged me up and threw a couple knees as he set me up for another suplex. This time I blocked him, and his second attempt as well. I shoved him off, and he bounced off the ropes before running back at me. I lunged at him in a football tackle known as a "spear" in wrestling. It didn't connect, as Tetsu leaped over me and I went down to the mat. I quickly got to my paws and ran at the ropes. I hit the ropes and turned back only to be met by Tetsu's signature move: a super kick he'd called *Kittsubusu* in Japan—the Fox Crush. It caught me under the jaw and, with a little help from me, lifted me off my paws.

I flipped over the ropes, falling to the padded floor, and I rolled to a rest in a sitting position at the barricade that separated the front row of the crowd from the action. I sat there stunned and waited for the world to stop spinning. My nose cap had parted ways from me, and the full array of smells in the arena hit me all at once, which did nothing to help my head. The crowd was cheering loudly now, and I could hear cries of "holy shit" mixed in. I felt the warm glow of pride and social acceptance in my chest. The referee began to count, and Tetsu pranced around the ring, daring me to come back in. I glared at him for the benefit of the camera-cat to my right before slowly getting to my paws.

The ref reached a count of six, and the crowd roared. I would just make it back in the ring in time. But at the count of eight, the growling British vocals of Duce's hard rock music hit. The cougar himself quickly appeared at top of the ramp.

"Stop the count!" he bellowed into the mic he was carrying as his music cut. "Stop the damn count!"

I staggered forward and rested against the ring apron as I looked up at the cougar. In the ring, Tetsu leaned over the ropes and threw his paws wide in a "what the hell" gesture. Duce glared down at me, then at Tetsu in the ring. In story, Duce doesn't care for me much. Like most wolves, I'm an outsider. I don't fit in his world, and like a "true" lone wolf, I hadn't even bothered to make an effort to fit in it. I flashed the former World Champion my best groggy shit-eating grin. Duce's scowl deepened, and the cougar's tail twitched in agitation as he stepped forward and brought the mic back to his muzzle.

"You two idiots think you can just waltz out here, hop in my ring, and just have a match any time you damn well feel like it?" Duce began to prowl back and forth on the stage. "Did you just forget whose place this is?"

I stood up fully, and rubbed my nose as I watched Duce as he adjusted his suit coat and tie. In the ring, Tetsu climbed up on a turnbuckle and took a seat on the top of it as he watched the cougar. The red fox smiled in a manner that bordered on arrogance. Duce bared his fangs at the fox.

"You might be able to get away with crap like this in Japan," Duce roared. "But not here! Here we do things right."

Duce pointed at the ring and then at me. He shook his finger and stamped his paw in frustration.

"You wanted a match at Fall Brawl?" Duce asked pointedly. "You and this clown here have got it! You two go on and on by this 'strong style' of yours, so you're gonna show it off. In a Last One Standing match!"

The roar from the crowd swallowed up any reaction Tetsu and I could have made, but my tail—which I'd been wagging in a cocky manner—went still. I had not been expecting that. A Last One Standing match had only one victory condition: beat your opponent to the point where they couldn't answer a ten count from the referee. It was a perfect match to show off strong style. I growled nervously and flicked my ears.

Duce smiled triumphantly and headed back behind the curtain. Tetsu's music began to play, and the fox posed in the ring while I staggered up the ramp, shaking a little as the nerves and adrenaline left me, and trying desperately to hide my smile. I waited in the darkened entryway just behind the curtain while the cheers slowly died away as Tetsu made his own way up the ramp.

Tetsu threw the curtain back, waited for it to settle behind him, took a quick look around, and then threw himself at me when he was sure no one else but Duce was there. I pulled him off his paws and held him close as I spun around. Our noses met briefly in our version of a kiss, and I quickly set him down. The tension I had felt at needing to be perfect began to drain away.

"We did it, *ani*!" Testu clapped his paws together.

"You certainly did," Duce put in as he stepped in clapped us both on the shoulders. "Now you just have to do it again. But I'm sure you can. Hit the showers: you two have earned it. Welcome to GCW, Tetsu."

With that, the cougar left us alone. We stood there for a while, feeling very proud of ourselves and looking forward to the show we would put on at Fall Brawl on Sunday.

We'd stolen one show, and I was damn sure we could steal that one too.

THE NEEDLE AND THE DEPARTED
Weasel

Weasel is a degenerate writer and the main dude of Weasel Press & Red Ferret Press. Author of a warm place to self-destruct, *and* We Live for Half-Moons, *he has published a few books with small presses. Weasel has had several encounters with wolves, the best one being an acquaintance who ate about as much tobacco as he does. Location of said wolf is no longer known, but he was last seen escaping imaginary ninjas in the desert.*

I lost my job a couple weeks back. Wasn't a bad gig, push papers and crunch numbers for college students that would never be able to handle the amount of loans they were given—and they never could. So many of them would blow it all on technology that wasn't class-related. The problem with taking out student loans is you think you're going to pay them back when you graduate. Well, you're not. Maybe some, but most will just remain in debt and indentured servitude forever. But that's how it goes. I never paid mine, so it never mattered to me. When they let me go, they had a team of people. I figured they were afraid of me. I kind of looked like a mean son of a bitch to them. Pure white fur, like blinding, like fluorescent light blinding. Imagine me sitting at a desk, buzzing—ZZZZZZZZZZZZZZZZZZZZZZ. Blinding fur and blue eyes—a tall son of a bitch, towering over everyone else with sharp teeth. Menacing ain't it? At least that's what I'm told. Wolves have always been feared in my office ever since the postman went off on everyone. But I kept to myself. Never bothered with anyone there. They were either afraid I'd bite, or got lost in the blue eyes. Everyone wants blue eyes; I never saw the appeal of them. Now my boyfriend's eyes, those were eyes to fawn over. Jasper was a slender cat, but his green eyes were completely green. Like forest green. Like they'll die if you chop down a tree. I got lost so many times in them eyes of his. Worked for the both of us; just wanted to make him happy.

I lost that gig due to making the wrong kind of errors. My boss was never comfortable with a gay dude in the office, and I didn't plan on hiding the fact that I had the hottest piece of ass waiting for me at home. So I got fired for being gay, essentially, and maybe a wolf. As I said, they were afraid. I thought of fighting it, but decided to move on to other things. That's when we decided to leave. It was Christmas. The snow was dancing in the wind, and he was staring out the window, just watching the flakes mingle with each other. His fur had more color then. I remember the gray glowed in the outside light. It was—

immaculate. Our lights were turned off, the heat was out, couldn't pay the rent until the next month, and the landlord was being an ass about it all. I remember he said he could forget the debt if Jasp performed for him, and I just about broke his nose. I could never whore my lover out. I at least have some morals to me, not a lot, but some. I wouldn't let him be broken.

He was staring outside as I was coming in the door after a day of interviews and no luck. I spent the last few dollars we had on a bottle of Hot Damn alcohol. Some Southern nonsense, 100% proof alcohol, enough to make the world dissolve for the night. When I saw him, I had to take a moment. I didn't want to ruin the glow. Maybe that was all in my head; sometimes, I can't tell the difference. We all go crazy from time to time. I was simply crazy in love with this cat. I set the alcohol down, ran up behind him, trying to be romantic. Hands smoothed over his hips, and I tried to steal a nuzzle, but he darted away. I still remember the bits of white and gray fur that mingled in the air as he pulled himself away. My tail whipped in mild surprise. He was not one for showing affection. He was evil and damned to the ribcage, but I loved him. He tore up the hell inside me, told it to get out, and buried himself there. He replaced it. He owned it. The nights we were cold and had nothing but each other to warm up to, he owned every bit inside me. It's not often to get a cat in love with a wolf. Societal normies say it's not meant to be, but if they only saw what I saw, they wouldn't say a damn thing.

He made me a new son of a bitch! Changed up my drinking habits and got me to quit smoking. He said I was killing myself with everything I partook in. I'd always respond with, "Hell baby, you know life's no fun without a few vices." He would roll his eyes as he threw away my pack of cigarettes. The Damned was the best brand out there. Couldn't get a better flavor of tobacco than something as degenerate as your death in a small box, and The Damned knew how to bring that flavor. We all know we're going to die, which was why I smoked in the first place. I'm already dying, let me live it up for a few years before the earth comes to swallow me back. No God in my mind, just the dirt—the soft, sometimes welcoming dirt. After all the years of breathing ash, it never affected my fur. I never knew how it stayed so white. Sometimes it'd blind me. I thought of dyeing it, but the cat wanted me to stay natural. He liked being buried in snow.

When he pulled away from me, my heart started to pound. He still allowed me to have my fun when I wanted. I caught his arm, and he swung around revealing little tears coming out of his eyes. A tropical storm was brewing and it caught me off guard. It was the first time in our relationship I still had the sweet smoke of The Damned in my pocket. When cravings flare up, it's hard to ignore. My body tensed up, and I grew anxious as I waited for him to start yelling at me, but I was only met with silence. My fur stood on edge, and the snow piled on outside. It piled high ready to burst into the street, much like we were ready to burst at each other. I thought of starting the conversation, a bit of "hey baby, what's going on?" You know the sweet talk, the chitter-chatter that soothed all the lovey-dovey souls out there. But before I could open my mouth, the cat opened his, "I fucked up, Rick." He didn't say anything else. Just, "I fucked up." The words piqued my curiosity. My ears fumbled around as they tried to decode the words. I wanted to know how I could help him. I needed to know how I could put the pieces back together. I could handle him screwing around out there. I could even handle it if they did it in our bed. Little things can be fixed. I just needed to know.

I stepped forward, tail slowly dangling back and forth, and that's when I noticed it, the needle hanging from the boy's arm—I knew he had a problem. The tears traveled far down his face, matted his fur, made him and ugly mess, but I pulled him in and said nothing. I didn't know what to say—or what to do for that matter. We had no money and with the cat using, we probably had less than I expected. God how I needed a smoke, right there, right then! I needed something to handle the situation; that's when I pulled out my cigs. I lit up while I held him in my arms. I knew I should have been stronger than that, but my brain was scratching with white noise and his sobs. My paws rubbed his back as I inhaled in my moment of weakness. I wanted to tell him it'd be alright, but nothing is ever truly alright.

It was at that moment, I heard a knock at our door. Who the hell would have knocked at our door this time of night? Jasper got his ass up and away from me. I tried to grip every last inch of his arm, and when I lost the feeling of his index finger, my heart howled. When I think back to it, I always see the fluster of gray and white lingering mid-air. My ears were muffled. The nicotine hadn't taken effect yet; the white noise was pounding. He tossed the needle to the side. I heard muffled thuds and clanks as he twisted the knob and opened the door. Our landlord stood in the door way, face like the devil, demeanor like his demons. The cat turned to me with a look of apology on his face and left.

Before that door closed, I got up off the ground and grabbed ahold of his arm, "You don't have to do this, baby! We can figure it out, even if we gotta sleep in the goddamn snow! We can figure it out!" He shrugged me off, kissed me on my bad side, and said he'd be back. He never came back.

Weeks after the incident, I got kicked out of the joint. The landlord couldn't wait to sell my stuff and get me outta here. Jasper had pretty much disappeared. When I asked the badger throwing me out where Jasp was, all he could say was, "I don't know, maybe getting his rocks off elsewhere." If the law would have allowed me to kill this man, I would have done it a long time ago. As he walked me to the front of the building, I spit on his shoes, told him I'd be back if Jasper was hurt—or worse.

When I went to the police, they didn't seem too concerned. They went through the general reports to fill and asked me when the last time I saw him was, you know how these things go. When they heard about the landlord and whatever was performed, they said they'd look into it. Was told that people go missing every day; that it wasn't unusual. When I left, I cussed those sons of bitchin'-ass eatin'-power hungry-bastards all the way down to the liquor store. Grabbed myself a bottle of bourbon and a pack of smokes. I was lost. I sat out at the subway and just watched people, figured if I stared at enough of them, he would appear. Every time a cat crossed my way, I perked up only to be disappointed in the end.

I was sitting around the subway one damn day. And the day was damned. When you walked outside, the clouds spat down droplets like the rich folk spit on poor folk. I encountered a fox begging for chump change—interesting fellow. I had never seen a purple-nosed, black-furred fella like him, so I slid up next to him. He wasn't too bad-looking, but he was no Jasper. I offered him what little I had of my bourbon and the bastard took the rest. We introduced ourselves; learned his name was Jimi, like the guitarist. I watched him dance, and we jabbered on cause we had nothing else to do. His hips swayed; nearly put a damn spell on me. I remember feeling my fur stand still when he twirled his tail and dropped his hips. If my heart weren't already dead, I'd have made a move. I remained silent. When he sat back down, he stared at me for a second. There was a curiosity in his eyes I couldn't quite read. I stared back at him, tail twitching in uneasiness, fur still on edge. I wish I could say I lost color, but when your fur is bleach white, you have nothing else to lose.

"Say man, what you doin' out here? Don't you got a home to get to, maybe a pretty little thing?" he asked amidst laughter.

I relaxed the tension in my muscles. I hadn't lost any definition in my body, but I knew if my hunger continued for anything longer, I'd become frail. I took out a smoke from my pack and told him my story. I needed the nicotine to keep the anxiety from pushing me in front of the subway. I told him about the landlord. I told him how lost I was, about how far away from heaven I fell when the cat left me.

He shared in a smoke with me before leaving. There was a silence between us for a few seconds. "I don't know if this'll help you, man, but there's this place on Jenner St. They got all sorts of drugs and heebie jeebie sexual nonsense. Your boy may be in there. I hope you find him…" and with that, he got up and waved goodbye. I watched the purple tip of his tail sway back and forth; he had a nice ass for a homeless dude. The news he gave me was probably the most I had gotten out of Jasper's disappearance.

I decided to take a look at this house. Jenner St. was not the best kind of place to be in. Up the road, there were groups of people fighting over nothing. Like an open fight club which I did not partake in. There was a house painted green when I got to the corner. Loud music was blaring from the garage as a group of kids were wandering out. An otter lowered the sleeves of his army jacket and walked up toward me. I caught his attention, and waved him over. Knelt down and asked him, "You seen this guy around, man?" When he didn't answer I dropped my last few dollars in his hand. "You seen him or not?"

He shook his head, "He no longer comes around. He didn't have any money for the juice so they drove him away."

A tiger from across the way was charging up. He was a rather large person, muscles bulging from the sleeves of his shirt, which read "People Hate Me." I could imagine why. I suppose he didn't like me talking with this kid, but I needed some kind of answer. Jasper was gone and ain't no one know where he went. I checked for the knife in my pocket and stepped back.

"Whoa, man. I don't want no trouble." I said as he walked up. He responded with a fist right into the sharp teeth sticking out from my maw. A tooth flies out as I'm pushed back by the force of this monster's strength. Goddamn, I had never been hit so hard in my life. I got back up and swung at his stomach. Punched him right in the gut, then landed a second one in the dude's neck. The tiger tried bobbing and weaving like a boxer, but once I caught his jaw he was too out of it. This massive beast fell back a little bit, coughing as I drove one last punch into his face to get him down. I spat out some blood, breath as heavy as all hell. I knelt down and pulled out a picture of Jasper again, "You seen this guy?" I asked him. He only responded with a nod. I was snarling by this point. Drool and blood meshing together on my fur. I don't know why he chose to fight me. Maybe just random aggression he needed to get rid of, or maybe he was too coked out of his mind. Either way, it was a fight he did not win.

The last of my leads began to trickle away as quick as they came. I started to believe I was never going to see that cat again.

I still dream of him at night. When I'm in the right alley, behind the right dumpster, I sit back and stare up at the cracks between the buildings. My heart is not yet ready to fall crooked for him; it's not ready to empty itself of Jasper—such a curse to be so obsessed with someone.

I remember our first argument. I forgot to bring the milk home, and he sky-rocketed from there. Words screaming and hollering in the apartment about how I don't listen and I'm so selfish and how dare I forget something so important…and I don't even know what I did except forget the milk. I was fortunate he wasn't someone who threw things. I locked myself up in the bedroom and let him cool off, listened to the Tailhole Surfers to drown out his bitching. I loved him.

While we were dating, I saw some guy giving him trouble. He was a slender kitten, not bad-looking, so many folks wanted a piece of his ass. This deranged Dalmatian dude was trying to pick him in this bar called Not's a couple years back. He got a little too touchy-feely for my comfort. Well, I came right up behind him and swung him around, told him to buzz off, he was my date for the night. When he waved me aside, I grabbed him by his shoulder and punched him in the jaw. I had never seen someone fall so easily. The guy was not sober by any means. I've always wondered what the guy could do if he were. If I'd be in the hospital—but that's all afterthoughts. Nothing important now.

Tonight, the city was alive. I was trying to get some sleep behind the Café Fin, but the drunkards were wandering the streets. A group of teenagers in Christmas sweaters just walked by, but there was a guy in the middle of them who looked too old to be there. He lifts up his pipe and lights up. A genuine way to smoke some good crack. Well, crack anyway, I wouldn't know what good crack is if you'll believe any of that. You won't believe what goes on in the city unless you just sit and watch. People are interesting souls.

I still see Jimi wandering around. He tells me he's moving onward though. This town's done him in, and it's just about time to get on elsewhere. I'm going to miss that hot piece of ass walking around, but I wished him safe travels, and we parted ways.

I suppose, some folks think I'd want to get back to workin. Get my own joint after being thrown out, and believe me, I know most would say evicted, but that bastard didn't evict us. He threw us out. No official notices, no police, just a get on out after he took Jasper from me. I've often pondered on the thought of murdering the bastard just to get some kind of satisfaction. Not revenge, but something to satiate my anger, then I take another swig of…I think I got scotch this time. I take another swig of the hard stuff and smoke another pack. I started panhandling, making decent cash each day. I've lost all my possessions, just carry around a CD player from a pawn shop and some old punk CDs. The punks know how to drive the anger out of a wolf, while inciting the riot in his heart. I can't tell you how many dumpsters I've ruined over the past couple weeks just getting drunk and kicking the shit out of them. It doesn't matter. When you lose everything you realize that nothing matters anymore. That all this, the jobs, the houses, it's all some weird façade we've grown into because we don't know anything else. We just know how to get ourselves ahead; how to use others and come out on top. This is all some big competition, and we'll do anything to win it, and I mean anything.

Across the café, there's a bar. That same group of Christmas sweater teenagers were dragging some poor guy out of it. A pack of generic grey wolves. And yes, I mean generic. Teenagers all copy each other, and these bastards all looked alike on purpose. I watched them take the guy into an alley. I couldn't see the victim too well, but I heard him scream. I heard him cry non-stop. "No, please, let me go!" Over, and over, and over, and these entitled bastards were just gonna rough the boy up, maybe put him on an online video of bum fights because the poor are entertainment to the entitled class. All ye men of high class and high cash, look upon your monuments and see how desolate you've become. I couldn't let this guy get pummeled. If anything I'd get my drunk-ass kicked as well, so I broke the bottle of scotch I bought and ran up to the first teenager I could and stabbed him right in the back. Right in his kidneys. I pulled out and pushed him aside. I started waving it around, slicing guys in the face like I would at the punk shows. You know the type, where you mosh with razor blades and get messed up while the music played. Tailhole Surfers would have been proud at this display. I sliced up whoever was in my way before those assholes ran off. They were too afraid of my attack. Didn't know how to handle the big bad white wolf coming for their stomachs! They ran so fast, they even left their friend there to bleed.

I toss my weapon in the trash and check on the guy. He's leaning over a pile of garbage, all beat up. I turn him over and that's when I see him—Jasper. My heart stopped. I could feel the one large thud crash against my rib cage as I see his broken body strung about the garbage. I start frantically throwing the bags away, hoping there were no needles. They beat him up bad, real bad. Bits of his fur were missing; I'm assuming from using too much. Heroin wouldn't do that unless you use the same vein over and over, at least that's what they show in the movies. I picked him up, blood was matted in his fur, some teeth missing, it wasn't good. His body was so weak, so cold, I wondered if he were alive at all. I ran, pushing more entitled assholes in my way. Three or four blocks later, I make it into the nearest emergency center.

They place him on a stretcher and lead us in.

The bed is just big enough for the both of us. The kitten sprawled himself as best he could on the surface while the machines attached to him beeped, blooped, and any other noise you could think of. As he lay there, I could only think of how pale his gray fur was, of how much the boy was dying. The nurses could only whisper about me, some arctic wolf come from up north.

They won't tell me anything. I'm not family, and we're not married. I lean in to nuzzle the ill kitten, wishing I had sealed our relationship. There is a bitterness to his scent, like stale medicine in brown bottles. White fur meshes with gray as I kiss his cheek; I don't bother to care if anyone was watching. Though I know I could be thrown out any minute, I take my chances; I take them for him.

Jasper never showed too much affection. He was just old enough to drink when I met him. The Flogged Foxes were in town, and I watched him from across the bar, downing six or seven shots of straight whatever. While the band played angrily in the background, I marked him as my prey. My tongue slid across my muzzle as I licked the last of my alcohol from my lips. Finished with my orders of scotch and bourbon, I caught the boy in a dance, and goddamn did we dance that night. Wolves are not notorious dancers, but when you're drunk enough, the floor is yours to own. Wolf and Cat twisting and jolting between drunk punk rockers looking to get laid, but it was worth it for him. The snow was mingling with the air outside, and we knew we'd have to walk out there cold. Though at that moment in time it didn't matter. When I swung him around to dance, he smirked so wide the devil would've been jealous.

The night I met Jasper was the night I would never be able to let go. We dated shortly after our dance. Though I can't remember what all happened that night, I'm pretty sure we went back to his apartment to "get to know each other better." Did we stop in the alley first? I can't remember, it's been so long ago. Time obscures everything. One thing it never changed was the fact that I loved him, as cheesy as that sounds. I loved him, and I followed him everywhere.

I hop in the bed with him while the nurses worry about other patients. They only come around every few hours. Though his scent remains bitter, I don't care. I nuzzle my face into his cheek, place my hand on his chest and feel the weak beat of his heart. It was the beat of a heart that had given up. I don't know what he did when he left me. I wonder if his heart had this beat to it when he left. How long had he been using? How long could he not trust me to help him? How long was I failing him?

It feels good to hold him again. I try not to move the wires. I just squeeze in on the side, a ball of white fluff trying to keep him alive, to keep him warm—to fix what I could not, maybe cannot, fix. His breath rattles. It's like he's a frog, croaking with each inhalation. I keep saying he'll be fine, but that rattle only means death is in our room. Nurses walk by as his rattling becomes more frequent. His breath is furious, he cannot breathe, but his heart does not change. It stays at the same beat as he struggles to stay here, stay with me. I can do nothing but kiss his cheek, and the moment I plant my lips on his fur, he stops. He just—stops.

WOLVES THAT SING
Billy Leigh

Billy Leigh is a grey, brown, and white Wolf who mostly likes to write stories from a historical perspective. He enjoys being a Wolf since he's a loyal and sociable individual. In particular, Billy likes spending time with his mate, hanging out with friends and going for long walks in the countryside or the forest near his house to get inspiration for new writing projects.

What did you do in the Second World War?

That's the question my grandcubs often ask me. I smile and tell them that I sang.

"Sang?" comes the reply. *"What, you didn't shoot anyone?"* Of course, they're too young to understand that's not the nicest question to ask, but I humor them and explain that I did carry a rifle, but I didn't shoot anyone. I sang in a troupe.

Since the start of the war, I kept a journal detailing all the locations I visited, and I guess the war enabled me to travel to different parts of the world. Writing my journal also helped me document the most amazing and frightening chapter in my life. It's an event that I'll never forget and a time that we proved singing wasn't just something you can do to entertain.

I was part of a small and unique squad of lupine troops. There's the picture of us; I'm standing on the far-left, the gray and white Wolf. Lieutenant William "Will" Evans is the black Wolf beside me. He was a celebrity and was already a well-known singer before the war broke out. Born in Wales, he is known for his deep tenor voice but also his distinctive howl. Find a record of his singing, and I guarantee the fur on the back of your neck will stand on end. Thomas Hawkins and Reg Thompson are the two white Wolves on the right. Our official title was the Entertainment National Services Association, but our little group was nicknamed the WTS, aka *Wolves That Sing*. We were flown to Europe and the Far East to entertain troops on the front line and established ourselves as a very popular act.

Despite this, we were all different in personality. Will was the leader of the pack, not just because he was famous and an officer, but also because he could stay calm at a time of danger. He was always a stoic and reassuring influence. Thomas was a private school boy, educated at a prestigious music college in London. Reg meanwhile was a cynical working-class lad from Manchester. I guess that's why Reg and Thomas kept fighting at first and Will acted as a mediator. I mostly kept to myself offstage, writing in my journal to document our various adventures, but I quickly established my position in the pack as the quiet one. Whenever Thomas and Reg got into a verbal dispute I stayed out of it, leaving Will to put a stop to it.

It reminded me too much of the fights my parents would have when I was a cub.

Despite our differences offstage, the act of performing stopped us from arguing. It's how Wolves always do things best, by working with their pack.

Together we made a powerful singing group. Thomas and I had deep, resonating voices while Reg and Thomas could hit the high notes. You'd think we wouldn't make the best singers when you hear a Wolf talk, but when a pack of Wolves howl in unison it can make the most chilling yet beautiful sound you'll ever hear. It's a sound that can bring tears to the eyes of the toughest of canines. We always howled to harmonize before we launched into song. At least a dozen times, we had people coming to us after a concert to say they thought the howling was on a record and were amazed it was actually us.

However, just because we weren't frontline troops did not mean we weren't under threat. Far from it. During some of our concerts we were shot from the air by our enemies or had to run for cover when artillery fire came raining down. The greatest time of danger we faced was performing on ships in the Far East. The Japanese would sneak up in their little submarines and sink British vessels without warning.

It was after such a concert when the event happened.

We'd performed in Ceylon for a group of drunken British sailors on board an aircraft carrier. I had been feeling apprehensive beforehand. I could hear the sailors whistling and hurling vulgar flirtations at a female Calico who was singing before us. As we lined up, took a deep breath and howled, the drunken chatter and laughing stopped. The audience then sat captivated for the next fifteen minutes and clapped their paws while howling for more once we finished.

"Gentlemen, we did it again!" Will noted proudly.

We left the ship feeling confident for our next concert which was to take place in Burma the following week, but as soon as we were on the dockside the bickering began, this time over a she-Wolf that Thomas and Reg had tried to flirt with.

"Hey, I had my eye on her first Thomas, you thieving git!"

"But I actually went over and spoke to her."

"She wouldn't want you anyway: you've probably got fleas since you never wash."

"The only thing I have, Reg, unlike you, is intelligence, and sadly for you that isn't contagious." I hung back and splayed my ears as I tried to block out the argument, until Will broke it up.

After being driven to an airfield, we boarded a little DC3 Dakota plane bound for India before we were going to take a train to Burma. The two Labradors flying the plane assured us we would arrive safely, especially considering we had the famous Will Evans on board.

The plane took off into the night and shuddered slightly in the wind. I didn't feel too bothered. The reaction we had gotten from the performance was still making my tail wag.

The little DC3 flew high above the sea. I glanced out of the window and marveled at the brilliant and dazzling sunset casting its light over the ocean. The tropical sunset was something that had been completely alien to me before the war. As a canine used to winter temperatures, it was such a sight to behold. A smile crept across my muzzle and thoughts of the war melted away.

The sun disappeared over the horizon, and the purple dusk set in. I felt tired, so I leaned back against the bulkhead as I listened to the thrumming of the engines. I pulled out my journal and began to write.

I was half aware of something crackling on the radio from the cockpit and the pilots chatting anxiously.

"Something wrong?" Will called.

"Japanese fighters have been spotted in this area," one of the Labradors shouted back. I put my journal back into my pocket as my ears perked up.

I gazed out of the window, but it was too dark to see anything outside.

I thought I heard one of the pilots curse, but before my mind could comprehend what was happening, something strafed along the side of the cabin. A bullet pierced the window and shot straight past my left ear. Had I been sitting an inch closer to the glass it would have taken my ear clean off.

Wind howled into the cabin, and I heard the engines wheeze and flame out. Before I knew it, we were all sliding out of our seats as the DC3 nosedived.

"Hold on chaps!" Will shouted as we all tried to grab hold of something.

The plane was spiraling out of control. I was pinned to the wall, unable to move. We were falling. I opened my muzzle to yell, but we hit the ocean's surface with a bone-shattering crash.

Black water rushed into the cabin, washing me out of my seat. I barely had time to scream before I was under. I knew I had to get out of the cabin immediately. Fumbling around with my seatbelt, I freed myself and began to swim upward. There was still a gap between the cabin ceiling and the rising water. I gasped for air and searched frantically around for my friends.

"Thomas, Reg, Will?" I shouted. "Are you there?"

"I'm over here!" Thomas sputtered as he surfaced. "We've got to get out of here before it sinks."

We swam toward where the cabin door had been.

"We've got to go underwater; can you swim?" I asked.

"Yes, just about," Thomas replied as he desperately trod water. The sea was almost up to our muzzles.

"We must go now, take a deep breath, try to keep your eyes open and follow me," I commanded. I sucked as much air as I could into my lungs. *Here goes nothing.*

I pushed myself under the water and kicked out with my hind-paws. I could faintly see the outline of the door and I swam toward it. I made it out of the plane and started to swim upward. Spying moonlight shining above, I made for it.

Breaking the surface, I gasped for air, kicking my hind-paws to stay afloat. The tail of the plane was still sticking above the surface. I watched with a heavy heart as it slid beneath the waves and disappeared.

"Thomas!" I called. A wave splashed into my mouth, filling my muzzle with salty water and causing me to choke. I felt a cold, sinking feeling in the pit of my stomach. There was no sign of any of my friends and without a lifejacket, I could soon tire and sink beneath the surface. The sun had completely set, leaving me alone in the middle of the dark sea.

Then, there was a splash beside me as Thomas surfaced and gasped for air.

"You made it!" I exclaimed as my tail thrashed around in the water.

"Yes, but where's Reg, Will, and the pilots?" he asked. My brief moment of joy turned to desperation again.

"Perhaps if we both howl, they'll hear us?" I suggested. I felt there was little chance of finding them if they didn't get out of the plane, but I wanted to do something before I gave up hope. Thomas and I raised our heads and howled at the sky. There was a moment of silence, but I couldn't believe my ears when I heard two howls coming out of the gloom.

"Over here," I said as I swam in their direction.

A warm sense of relief rushed over me as I saw Will and Reg sitting on a yellow inflatable raft.

"You made it too!" I gasped as I hauled myself onto the raft.

"We thought you two were gone," Will replied as he helped us on board. I patted my pocket and realized my pen and journal were still there, and in one piece. Some of the pages were stuck together but miraculously the ink hadn't run.

"Where are the pilots?" I asked. Will and Reg didn't say anything but exchanged a sad glance that answered my question. I sighed and gazed regretfully over the water.

I shivered in the night air as my damp clothes clung unpleasantly to my fur. The other three had their muzzles pointed down and their ears splayed.

"We're alive," Will said. "All we need now is for someone to rescue us."

"But where are we?" Reg sighed. "I wasn't following the route they were flying us. If no one finds us, we're going to die of dehydration."

"We'll be fine," Thomas asserted. "If we wait 'til dawn and see a ship, we'll signal to it."

"With what exactly?" Reg snapped back, "and what if the ship turns out to be a Jap one?"

"Well what do you want to do? Sit here and complain about waiting to die, or signal to a ship and panic about the fact it may be Japanese?" Thomas growled.

"We're dead either way!" Reg exclaimed.

"Listen, listen!" Will cut in. "We won't get anywhere by fighting each other. We are Wolves; we stay together in our pack. Now, Reg is right. If we stay in the raft, we have no clean water or food, but if a ship comes into sight I think we should try our chances with it."

Will turned to me. "What do you think?"

I hesitated as I mulled our predicament over. It seemed I was damned either way, as I feared Reg or Thomas would snap at me whatever decision I chose.

"Will is right," I eventually said. That seemed to settle the matter, but we were left drifting aimlessly throughout the night.

The four of us sat in silence, occasionally wringing our tails out or shaking ourselves dry. The waves lapped against the side of the raft, and I was thankful we hadn't crashed during a storm.

Will suddenly sat bolt upright with his ears cocked. I followed his eyes and saw what looked like the lights of a ship in the distance. It looked like a small patrol vessel. My throat felt horse, but I tried waving and shouting. My three friends joined in.

"Hey! Hey! We're over here!" we chorused. The lights slid by as we continued waving and shouting.

"They can't hear us," Reg sighed.

"Keep shouting," Thomas replied. We kept calling but it was no use. Our voices slowly trailed off as the lights disappeared into the night.

We sunk back down in the raft and growled in unison.

"Well that didn't work," Reg muttered.

"It was better than doing nothing," Thomas replied. Reg's hackles were raised, and he bared his teeth at Thomas.

"They didn't see us because it's dark; we'll have a better chance at daybreak," I found myself saying. Will had opened his mouth to say something, but instead, he nodded in agreement.

"He's right. We'll hang on until daytime and wait until another ship passes."

We returned to silence. I knew I had to sleep, and Will seemed to read my mind.

"Why don't two of us sleep while two others keep watch?" he suggested.

I awoke to see the sun rising over the horizon. In spite of our predicament, I took a moment to admire the sight; the seemingly thousands of shades of red, orange, and yellow reflecting in the water was quite a sight to behold. Will and Reg were already awake while Thomas stirred and yawned.

"I don't suppose breakfast is out of the question?" he asked. Will and I laughed whereas Reg huffed to himself.

The raft was at the mercy of the sea-current. Twice we tried putting our paws in the water to paddle, but it was no use.

I sat upright. There was something on the horizon that looked like a boat, and we were drifting toward it. I remembered the patrol boat we had seen last had cruised in the same direction. It had to be them.

"Look!" I shouted. We all exchanged excited glances before we began waving and yelling. The gray outline of the patrol boat was getting closer.

"Why aren't they responding?" Thomas said as he turned to shoot us a worried glance. As we drifted closer my heart plummeted.

"Wait, that's not right," Reg whispered to himself.

The patrol boat was capsized and surrounded by a pool of burning oil. We gazed grimly at the sight as the raft drifted by. There was no sign of life. We called out, but no one responded. We allowed the current to take us away as we watched the hull disappear beneath the waves.

A horrible thought occurred to me; if the patrol boat had been on our side then whoever had attacked it was still lurking somewhere nearby. We gazed out at the water with our ears perked up, but whoever had sunk it seemed to have disappeared.

We continued drifting for what felt like several hours in silence. There seemed to be nothing around us. The blue ocean stretched into the distance to the point where it merged with the sky. As a cub, I'd often pretended to be a pirate or proudly told my mother I would sail the seven seas. She'd laugh and tell me I was a land canine, not a sea dog. The sight of the endless sea turned the memory sour.

"Well, this certainly looks nicer than looking out at the North Sea during winter," Thomas chuckled.

"It's still water, just a different bleedin' color," Reg grumbled. I sensed things were going to get tense.

"Why don't we sing?" Will suggested. The other two exchanged looks.

"I'm not sure we should use up our energy," Thomas sighed.

"I think we could use a morale boost," Will replied. "Plus I don't want our practice to lapse while we're floating out here. Let's do *The White Cliffs of Dover.*"

We opened our muzzles and began to harmonize. Even out at sea our voices sounded resonate and powerful. We howled in unison before we began to sing.

Even lost at sea, the sound of the song elevated my spirits. I'd been told at a young age that Wolves harmonize to create the effect that there are more of us than there really are, something that stemmed back to Cave-Wolves hunting their prey. I could hear it then in our voices as we drifted along.

Once the song was over we laid back in the raft, panting. I could see smiles on their muzzles and felt happy they'd been as uplifted by the song as I had.

"Hey, over there!" Thomas shouted as he gestured to something on the horizon. We all followed the direction of his paw and saw an island in the distance. The current was taking us toward it.

The island looked like something from a postcard; white sandy beaches, palm trees and blue lagoons in the rocks. I took stock of our surroundings as the raft washed up on the beach.

"Perhaps there's someone here who could help us?" Thomas mused.

"If they're not the enemy," Reg huffed. Will climbed out of the raft and scratched his muzzle as he came to a decision.

"Right, Thomas you come with me to search the East side of the island. You two search the West, and then we'll meet back here in twenty minutes," he commanded.

We split into our search parties, and I walked along the sand with Reg in tow.

"What if the enemy is here?" Reg repeated in a whisper. He was starting to unnerve me, so I reached down and picked up a heavy branch lying in the sand. I knew it wouldn't do me a lot of good if we ran into a group of Japanese troops with guns, but it felt faintly reassuring to carry it. Reg gave me a withering look.

"Well, what will you use if they attack us?" I asked.

"My teeth!" Reg replied as he growled and bared his fangs. I wanted to point out that teeth were no match for rifles either but decided to keep my muzzle shut.

The island consisted of sand with a dense patch of vegetation in the middle. The heat of the morning sun felt almost unbearable against my coat of fur. We'd had our pelts trimmed short back in England, but mine always grew back quickly. My tongue was hanging out as I panted and forced myself through the undergrowth. I hoped to come across any sign of life for friendly locals; a road or a hut. A couple of exotic-looking birds squawked up ahead but aside from that, there was no sign of life. I sniffed about, but I couldn't smell the scent of any other canines, friends, or foes.

I was still feeling hot and drowsy by the time Reg and I made our way back to the beach. I paused and gazed at one of the lagoons. The water looked so cool and inviting. I bent down to lap some up but instantly spat it out and wretched. It was salty and revolting. I could immediately see why no one was living on the island.

We regrouped back by the raft, and Will explained the West side of the island was uninhabited too.

"We did find trees that seem to be growing coconut," Thomas explained. "At least we won't starve." The coconuts turned out to be well out of the reach of our paws up trees that looked impossible to climb.

"And how do you propose we get up there?" Reg sighed. "They're far too tall."

"It's either try climbing that or go hungry," Thomas replied.

"Well, would you like to stand on my shoulders or do you have a step ladder stashed in the bush?"

"Enough!" Will barked, "I'll climb the tree. I used to do this as a cub at my grandmother's house."

The three of us watched as Will shimmied up the trunk.

"He should have been born a feline," Thomas chuckled while Reg watched in disbelief as Will made it to the top. He turned and waved to us as we clapped our paws.

"Nothing to it!" Will laughed. He reached out and grabbed a coconut in his paw.

"Come on you bugger," he growled as he tried to shake one loose.

"Are they ripe enough yet?" Thomas shouted.

"Don't worry, it just needs a good, firm…" Will was in mid-sentence when he lost his grip and fell. He didn't have time to cry out before he hit the ground with a sickening *thud*.

To my shame, I initially thought the scene looked like something from a slapstick comedy, expecting Will to jump back up.

He didn't.

The three of us crouched down.

"Will, are you all right?" I asked, thinking the question sounded silly and unhelpful. Will groaned and tried to get up but winced in pain.

"My hind-paw is broken," he groaned through gritted teeth.

"Stay on the ground and don't move," I advised.

The three of us consulted amongst each other and decided to carry Will down to the beach before Thomas and I went to look for firewood.

We sat by the fire in silence. I watched the flames dance as the sound of crackling filled the night air. Thomas and Reg were bickering quietly but their voices soon grew louder.

"You shouldn't have encouraged him to climb the tree."

"Me? He did it himself."

"Enough!" I cut in. Both Wolves turned to face me with expressions of surprise.

"He spoke," Reg marveled.

124

"We aren't going to get anywhere by fighting each other; we're pack canines," I continued. "We've got two choices: one of us can wait here with Will while the other two take our chances in the raft to look for help, or we can all get in the raft together" I explained. Thomas and Reg muttered amongst each other as they considered what I'd said.

"We'll decide by sunrise when we can see well," I eventually said. "In the meantime we'll get more firewood."

Reg and Thomas promised they'd stop arguing and would go to get more branches while I stayed with Will. The black Wolf was sleeping so I pulled out my journal to keep writing. Call me selfish, but I wanted to keep it hidden in case we couldn't find any more firewood and the others wanted to use it as kindling. With Will out of action, I needed to assume his leadership style to keep our pack together.

The other two came hurrying back down the beach with no firewood in their arms. I was about to call out, but Thomas put a finger to his muzzle and sprinted over to me.

"Another boat has landed on the island; they're Japanese," he panted.

"Are you sure?"

"Certainly, we could hear them talking," Reg added.

"Right, we need to leave. You two get the raft ready, and I'll wake Will," I whispered. I scooped up as much sand as I could in my paws to dowse the fire.

I sprinted over to where Will was sleeping and gently shook him.

"Will? We need to leave." I whispered urgently into his ear.

"Wha...what?" he whispered back.

"C'mon," I muttered as I tried to help him up. Will winced and yelped as he stood on his bad hind-paw. I cursed, hoping none of the enemy had heard us.

"Here," I whispered as I helped the black Wolf over my shoulders. I staggered back down to the beach to see Thomas and Reg about to push the raft back out to sea. I heaved Will into the back and climbed aboard as we pushed off into the waves. We paddled as hard as we could with our paws. I could hear the sound of shouting behind us, and I risked a glance back to see several dark figures running down the beach.

"Paddle faster!" I breathed as we splashed against the tide. I heard the *crack* of a rifle being fired. A bullet whipped past my head, but we kept paddling without looking back.

Eventually, I turned my head to see that the island had almost disappeared into the night. No one had tried pursuing us out to sea. I slumped back in the raft and sighed with relief.

We kept drifting with the current until the dawn arrived. The morning sun was blazingly hot, and our throats felt parched. I pulled off my shirt in an effort to feel cooler, but there was no escape from the sun. Will was lying on the bottom of the raft, drifting in and out of consciousness. The three of us tried to shield him from the sun with our bodies. I gazed out at the sparkling blue sea water as I thought of a rhyme about the sea my mother had taught me as a cub.

Water, water all around, and not a drop to drink.

The blue nothingness taunted me as the words continued to plague my mind.

"We're all going to die; we're all going to die," Reg chuntered to himself.

"We're not going to die," I replied firmly.

"Want to bet?" he replied as he gestured toward a patch of ominous black clouds forming on the horizon. My heart plummeted, but I put on a brave face for the rest of my pack.

"Well, it seems we're sailing towards it lads," I announced. "Hold on tight and make sure Will doesn't fall out." I leaned down to the semi-conscious black Wolf in the bottom of the raft.

"We're about to hit a storm, but we'll hold on," I assured him. Will didn't seem to understand what I said, but he smiled cheerfully back. I sighed and gritted my teeth.

The wind was starting to ruffle my fur, and the sky was growing darker by the second. There was an odd calm in the air, but I knew all hell was going to break loose soon.

The rain came first. It's not like the pattering rain that falls in England; this hit us like a hail of bullets. Within seconds my fur was sodden and plastered to my face. The raft was filling up at an alarming rate.

"Reg, keep Will's head above water; Thomas help me bail out!" I shouted above the racket. A violent wind had picked up, and waves were soon crashing into the raft. Thomas and I frantically tried to bail out the water with our paws, but as soon as we got one load out a wave would bring more crashing in.

The wind grew ever more powerful, and the raft rocked from side to side as water sloshed about inside. Reg cursed under his breath as he tried to keep Will's head from going under.

"I'm not sure I do this!" he cried.

"You can!" I called back. "We'll make it." The words had barely escaped my muzzle when, as if by some cruel joke, a freakishly large wave capsized the raft. We were catapulted into the churning water. I flailed about with my arms and kicked with my hind-paws until I reached the surface. I glanced around frantically and saw Thomas sitting on the upturned raft.

"Over here!" he called as I swam over. He grabbed my arms and hauled me up.

"Where's Will and Reg?"

"Here!" Reg spluttered as he trod water while keeping Will afloat with one arm. Thomas reached down and hauled Will aboard as Reg followed.

"I made it. I got him!" Reg exclaimed. Despite the situation, I was impressed.

"Splendid, now we just have to stay out of the water," I shouted above the wind.

Reg and I held onto Will as the upturned raft was battered by the waves, but as quickly as the storm arrived, it disappeared.

The sea calmed itself, and the light of the hot sun pierced through the black clouds.

"You did well there Reg," I said as I shot him a smile.

"Thanks," he replied as his tail thumped against the raft, "but I couldn't have done it without Thomas."

The clouds had completely vanished. The endless blue sky reappeared, and while I'd have normally found such a sight beautiful, I knew it would soon become unbearably hot. Some rain water had collected in the folds of the raft, and I leaned down to lap some up before gesturing to Reg and Thomas to do the same. I scooped some up in my paws and held it to Will's muzzle.

"Here," I whispered as I tipped the water into his open mouth.

"You know, when we get off this raft, I could do with a nice pint of ale," Reg sighed.

"I'd like a dance with Greta Garbo," Thomas grinned. "What would you like, Will?"

"A bowl of butterscotch pudding," the black Wolf murmured. The other two laughed.

I didn't take part in the conversation as I'd seen something that made my heart skip a beat.

A ship on the horizon. I strained my eyes and saw it was sailing in our direction.

Without saying a word, I extended a paw and pointed. The others followed my gaze and began wagging their tails and chattering excitedly.

"Wait, what if it's a Japanese ship?" Reg asked. I paused as I considered his point.

"All right, we've got two options. Either we let the ship pass, or we take our chances."

Thomas and Reg looked at each other before turning back to me.

"Let's take our chances," they both said in unison.

We began waving our paws and shouting.

"Hey! Hey!" We chorused. The ship sailed closer, but I couldn't see any hands on deck pointing back in our direction.

"We need a flag or something," Thomas said as he glanced around frantically, as if trying to pull one out of thin air. The ship was getting closer and I could see it was a destroyer of some sort. I crawled across the upturned raft, trying to get a better look.

I felt such a wonderful sense of elation as I saw a Union Jack flying from the stern. An absurd grin spread across my muzzle.

"Keep shouting, it's one of ours!"

We kept shouting and waving, but still, no hands appeared on the deck.

"Sing!" I shouted. "Let's all howl and sing."

We raised our muzzles as we howled and harmonized in unison. The chilling yet ethereal sound filled the air.

"After three!" I called. "One, two, three…"

I closed my eyes and sang as loud as I could, howling in-between verses. The other two copied my example, and on the floor of the raft, Will stirred and opened his eyes. His tail thumped against the surface as he hoarsely joined in.

I opened my eyes again and saw to my amazement that the ship was turning in our direction.

Warm relief rushed over me when I saw a gray Wolf lean over the railing to glance into the raft.

"I'd recognize that kind of howling anywhere," he said with a grin. "They're down here, a raft full of Wolves!" he called to a crewman standing somewhere behind him.

We were hauled aboard the ship and taken to the medical bay.

"Is *that* Will Evans?" I heard some of the sailors murmur as the black Wolf was carried along the deck in a stretcher.

"Make way! Make way!" the Border Collie serving as the ships medical orderly barked.

Will was taken behind a curtain while we were told to sit outside before the Collie returned to treat us for sunstroke and dehydration. Normally, I found a ship's medical bay to be cramped and stark places, but at that moment I felt glad to be in something that felt solid and sturdy compared to the flimsy raft.

"Is he all right?" I asked nervously.

"He has a nasty bump on the head, and he's pretty dehydrated like you are, which certainly didn't help, but he'll pull through," the Collie explained. The three of us let out a sigh of relief.

"You don't happen to have a pen or pencil on you?" I asked, as mine had been lost in the storm. The Collie returned a moment later with a pen, and as we waited, I pulled out my journal and frantically wrote down all that had happened.

I figured that someday, someone might find it fascinating that I was lost at sea with Will Evans, but as I wrote, the importance of emphasizing our pack nature to help each other out became more of a feature.

Had I been stranded alone, I probably wouldn't have made it.

Eventually the medical orderly reappeared and called Reg to follow him, followed by Thomas five minutes later.

"Will has regained consciousness and wants to talk to all you," he explained, "but only one at a time please." When my turn came I put down my journal and followed the Collie through medical bay. Will was lying in bed, but he shot me something close to a grin as I walked over.

"I wanted to say good job on what you did; getting us rescued was quite an amazing thing to do, let alone stopping Thomas and Reg from fighting," he whispered.

"Thank you."

"No, thank you," Will said firmly.

Will was released from the medical bay a week later, with a warning not to climb any trees in the near future. We made it to Burma in time to sing at our next concert, this one performing for troops who had just come back from fighting in the jungle. I could tell by the grim looks on their faces they had had a tough time. I could sympathize, but as I remembered how singing had uplifted our spirits, I wanted to do the same for them.

The four of us opened our muzzles to harmonize, and I put everything I could into our performance.

We launched into the song, and I opened an eye to see the audience watching with a mixture of contentment and awe. I smiled inside as we continued singing.

As always, we impressed the audience who called out for more. As the audience clapped and cheered, I exchanged a glance with Will, Thomas, and Reg.

"Gentlemen, we did it again." Will grinned.

Singing together suddenly felt a lot more special.

INSTINCT
Faolan

Faolan is a tall young black wolf from the south of the Netherlands. His writing powers are strongest on the nights of the full moon, when he keeps to his den to provide entertainment for others, which includes, but is not limited to, dancing, singing, and telling stories to those who intend to watch and listen. Previously published in Seven Deadly Sins *by Thurston Howl Publications.*

"Thank you, sir, for that—ahum—overly-detailed information some of us did not need!"

The audience burst out in laughter, sending Minkyu's heart into overdrive while he was waiting backstage for his cue. He was trembling on his feet as the soundwaves washed over his ears. He fidgeted with his leather jacket, checking his outfit once more, to try to calm himself down. The black wolf looked back at the others of his group, who looked remarkably calm compared to him. He let out an anxious sigh and closed his mossy green eyes for a moment, moving his sensitive wolf nose up in silent prayer. The scents of dozens of different species assaulted him as a special perfume that could only be created by stuffing as many people as possible in a small area. The venue they were about to perform on was nowhere near as big as the stage they'd find themselves on in just a few weeks' time. Why was he so nervous about something like this? It was not as if his future depended on it. Well, okay, maybe a little.

Minkyu was startled slightly at the feeling of a paw landing on his shoulder. He turned around to look right into the amber eyes that belonged to Seojun.

"You're too tense. We'll be fine. We have worked hard for this, hyung," the skinny gray wolf said before nodding once.

His friend's assurance caused some of the tension to leave his body. Unfortunately, it came right back the moment the show host called them onto the stage.

"Now, ladies and gentlemen, taking the stage next is a wonderful new group of people who are fighting their way towards their debut. This is their first TV performance, but they are ready! Please, give it up for INSTINCT!" the dapper fox announced before walking to the side, making way for the group of five fresh new idols to take the stage.

Minkyu slapped his own cheeks before walking onto the stage wearing a tough and slightly angry look on his face. He moved his mic to his muzzle and raised his paw up into the air as soon as the other members had taken up their positions. "Good evening, Korea! We are INSTINCT! Fasten your seatbelts," he said before grinning into the camera that was pointed at him. The audience cheered and whistled their appreciation before they got quiet at the visual cue, filling the room with the crowd's anticipation. The music started playing a few seconds later

Minkyu started singing, his low voice easily reaching the hearts of the audience while the other members danced behind him and provided backup vocals. He spun around, moving back, while the two white wolves moved to the front. Yujin and Kiha, twins, were amazing dancers, and they could hit some amazingly high notes without a problem. Their identical voices made sure that they were an absolute delight to listen to. They danced perfectly as usual and played a prank on Minkyu, pulling up his shirt to reveal his abs for a second, before moving to the sides to make way for the rapper, Junyoung. The brown wolf had no problem flirting with the camera while rapping, even blowing a kiss before joining the group choreo. Strong bass fueled their dance parts, and the singing was absolutely flawless. The song went on for a few minutes before they struck their end poses and received the loud applause given by the audience and the people backstage. They bowed respectfully before leaving the stage.

The backstage crew greeted them with compliments and thanks before sending them to their dressing room. Water was provided for them, as well as some healthy snacks. They were sweating a little, and they slumped down on the various chairs and benches in the small room, panting softly for a minute or two, before the wonderful silence was broken.

Seojun leaned forward, turning his calm gaze upon the brown wolf on the chair opposite him. "Junyoung, your dancing lagged slightly behind in the fast part after your rap. Please, do better next time," he said calmly.

The other canine frowned, and his ears swiveled back before they went down. "I'm sure I don't know what you're talking about, hyung. I was completely in sync with the rest of you."

"I wish it were so, but you were throwing off our carefully constructed harmony. It's an important part in the dance that has to be perfect."

The younger wolf jumped up from his chair and growled at the lead choreographer. "It was fine!" he protested, his fur bristling.

"I will watch the video with you and give you a few pointers to make it perfect. Don't worry," Seojun said, keeping his calm eyes on the temperamental wolf in front of him. The gray wolf was the embodiment of serenity. Nothing could ever really throw him off. Junyoung, on the other hand, was just about to lose it. He still couldn't handle critique well, it seemed.

The leader stood up with a sigh and stepped between the two of them, flexing his muscles nonchalantly to make himself look bigger. "Alright, break it up, you two. We did a fine job out there, and we will do even better next time. Junnie, you absolutely nailed your rap again. Who cares about an almost invisible mistake in the choreo?" he said while smiling, moving an arm around his friend's shoulder before turning to Seojun. "Seojun, would you please analyze the video for anything we'll have to tweak?" he asked with a kind smile.

The brown wolf blushed and pouted a little. "Please, don't call me Junnie, hyung. Especially not when others are present," he said while calming down at the same time, the fur in his neck going flat again.

The choreographer nodded and looked away before drinking some more water.

"Great! Thanks for the hard work, guys! It's time to go back!" Minkyu announced before slapping Junyoung on his shoulder and ushering the others out of the dressing room. He looked at the twins, his gaze lingering on the younger of the two, Yujin. He smiled at the young wolf and was rewarded with a brilliant smile and a wink, causing the black wolf to blush, which, luckily, couldn't be seen due to his thick black fur. Both wolves were wagging happily for a few seconds, before the white wolf joined his twin outside. Minkyu made sure they left no mess behind before leaving the building with the others, where they were picked up by one of the agency's drivers, and brought back to said agency. Another successful show, another successfully-defused fight.

The next morning announced itself way too early through the sound of his alarm going off. The black wolf groaned and sleepily lifted his head from the pillow, forcing himself up on all fours before crawling over to the side of the bed and reaching out for the trousers he had been wearing the evening before. He couldn't exactly reach it, and, since pouting wouldn't work, he half-climbed out of bed and pulled the piece of clothing into the warm confines of his bordeaux sheets. Meanwhile, the cheerful tune of one of his favorite songs kept playing. Minkyu took the phone out of his trousers, shut it off, and sighed as he sat up and rubbed his eyes. Perhaps it wasn't such a great idea to pick a nice song as his alarm tune. He was starting to dislike it more every morning. The large wolf pushed himself up out of bed and stretched out his lovely toned body, popping a few joints, before walking out of his room, stark naked.

On his way to the showers, he came across Junyoung, who pretended to swoon and fanned himself, obviously putting on an act to tease his group leader about his nonchalance.

"Whew, Minkyu-hyung, how can you do this to me this early in the morning! My poor heart!" he said with a higher voice than usual and a huge grin on his face, his tail wagging in obvious joy.

The group's leader grunted his protest and playfully punched the other canine's shoulder as he walked past him and into the bathroom. They were all quite comfortable being naked around each other. They were five guys living in one apartment, so it was only natural that they'd gotten used to each other over time. At least they all had their own rooms, which were the only places where there was real privacy, the toilet being an obvious exception of course.

He turned on the warm water and sighed happily as it rained down on him and washed away his grogginess. Minkyu loved starting and ending his day with a shower, but he'd been too tired to shower the night before. He ran his paws over his hard body and washed himself thoroughly before just standing there, enjoying the feeling of the water finding ways through his fur as it streamed down. He forced himself out of the shower after a while and walked over to the full-body dryer, which dried his midnight fur within minutes.

After getting dressed into a comfortable tank top and sweat pants, the black wolf joined the rest of INSTINCT in the lounge area, where they always ate their meals. The rest, even Seojun, who was known for sleeping in, was already there and greeted him warmly. Kiha was working on breakfast, which was one of his duties in the house.

"Good morning, hyung. How would you like your eggs?" the small white wolf asked while smiling pleasantly.

"Good morning, Kiha. Scrambled please," he said before sitting down on one of the luxurious couches, sharing it with Seojun.

"Coming right up! Could you share today's schedule with us, glorious leader?" the cook asked while grinning a little.

Minkyu rolled his eyes and chuckled. "Of course, my loyal minion. Today, Kiha, Seojun, and Junyoung will practice their singing parts for our latest song. Junyoung, I expect your rapping to be absolutely flawless by the end of the day, but I'm sure you've got that covered," he said.

The rapper nodded and grinned, winking at the large wolf. "You got it, boss."

"Great! It seems Yujin and I are tasked with writing lyrics for a new song. The agency has sent us the instrumental version of the song we voted on last week, so we can finally get started on that. We should start on choreo for it as well soon. I will leave that to you, Seojun," he said. "This will be the song that will launch us right to the first place in the upcoming competition, so let's work hard on it!" he said while smiling.

The rest let out their own cries of approval, ate their breakfast happily, and went their own ways to work on their assignments. The youngest member, the maknae, joined the oldest in the writing room, which was decorated with cool posters of both landscapes and famous artists to inspire them in their songwriting. Minkyu was glad to have some alone time with the cute young wolf, both for selfish reasons, and because the maknae almost never spoke his mind in a group, unless someone specifically asked for his opinion. Yujin was wearing tight gray skinny jeans as well as a form-fitting black shirt. The silver rings in his ears completed the look that Minkyu quite openly admired, until the young wolf actually snapped his fingers in front of his nose, bringing the black canine back to reality.

"Huh?"

"You were spacing out again, hyung. It's quite cute, but we're supposed to be working, remember?" Yujin asked before giggling.

Minkyu blushed and nodded. He set up the laptop and writing gear before opening up the group's e-mail. He was the only one in INSTINCT who knew the password, since he was the one responsible for all communication between the group and the agency. He downloaded the song to the desktop and played it, letting his fellow writer hear it again. It was a very powerful and dark song with a very clear part for rapping and some space for the twins' lovely high notes. Minkyu had some ideas for the arrangements already, but he wanted to know what Yujin thought first. After the song was finished, he asked the wolf's opinion.

"So, I have some ideas for it already. What do you think, Yujin?" he asked.

The young wolf thought hard for a moment, placing a finger on his lips, as was his habit, before carefully answering.

"Well, the rap parts are quite clear, but it's a bit long. Perhaps we could have two people rapping in that part?" he suggested before continuing. "I thought the high notes would be great for the chorus, while the lower voices would be good for the other parts. The actual lines can't be divided among us until we have actually written them though," he said and smiled.

The black wolf clapped the white one on his back and pulled him in for a hug for a moment. His chest swelled with pride. Seeing the musical genius of the young canine was always amazing. He personally thought Yujin was better at this than he was, but he wouldn't tell him that, out of fear of ruining the boy's modesty. There was one thing that surprised and worried him about what he had said though.

"You and I are almost completely in sync! But eh…two rappers? And who do you suppose will be able to do that?" he asked.

"Well, I was thinking that maybe you would want to give it a shot. You're supposed to be the tough guy in our group, and rapping is the perfect way to show that."

"But I have never rapped before!"

"Exactly. It's a great way to expand your skillset, surprise the fans and staff, and you have the perfect voice for it, I think. Junyoung has a high rapping voice, so your low voice should complement his well. I have faith in you, hyung!" the cute wolf said with a bright smile on his face that Minkyu just couldn't ignore.

"Well, I guess we could give it a try," he said softly before jotting down a few notes. He supposed that Yujin had a point about his voice and image. He just hoped that he would actually be able to do a good job at it. Perhaps some one-on-one training with Junyoung would be a good idea. They spent the rest of the time working on possible lyrics, leaving the rap lyrics to their lead rapper, before joining up with the others for dinner and dance practise. They couldn't start working on the new dance yet, because their choreographer loved working with the lyrics and would wait for them to be done. Instead, they stuck to their usual repertoire.

"Again! Slide, jump, bounce, bounce, step, step, hit!" Seojun ordered as he counted along with the music. He was walking around the group to spot any mistakes they made. "Minkyu-hyung, more power!" he said as he replayed the music and started over again.

Minkyu frowned for a second before throwing in even more power than before, really pushing his body to the limit with his moves. They had been practicing for at least an hour already, and he was exhausted. Still, Seojun wouldn't let up.

"Again!"

The black wolf sighed and danced along with the others again, trying to keep his energy up. Seojun was a stern teacher, but he made sure that their dances were as spotless as they could possibly be.

"Yujin, bigger arm movements! That's it!"

Looking at the white wolf from behind, Minkyu couldn't see what exactly Seojun meant. Yujin's movements looked fine to him, but he was sure that there had to be something he hadn't seen. They kept on going for another three times before they could finally take a break.

The dancers either sat down or lay down on the floor, panting like rabid dogs and draining their water bottles. Dance training was always the hardest and most rewarding of their different training routines. It kept them all in perfect shape too. There was something really great about working on your body in a fun way, while also creating something from scratch.

"Alright, break time is over! Let's go over it again from the top!"

Minkyu flopped down on his bed after that incredibly tiring training session. He felt extremely dirty and started pulling off his sweaty clothes. That sure was one thing evolution had done totally wrong. Perhaps it was their own fault for putting on clothing though. He moved through his room and gathered his shower supplies before leaving for his second trip to the showers that day.

His ears perked up at the sound of a shower running as he walked toward the door leading into the shower area. He wondered who was using it at this hour. Most of the others only used the shower in the morning, so it was a mystery to him. The wolf hung up his towel and entered the room. After blinking a few times to get his eyes used to the humid air, he spotted a familiar white figure washing himself. Yujin. The black wolf's green eyes were glued to the slender wolf's beautiful figure, resting on his curvy hips and rump. He swallowed once and blushed while wagging a little.

"See something you like?"

He snapped out of his trance and looked up to see the smaller wolf looking at him with a mischievous smile on his face. "What?" he asked softly before moving closer. "I eh…I was just admiring how incredibly clean your white fur is. It has to be a real pain in the ass to keep it that way."

Yujin nodded and stroked his chest as he washed himself. "Yeah, but I'm used to it, so I guess it doesn't really bother me that much. It's annoying how quickly it gets dirty though," he said. His paws moved down to his stomach and hips, drawing Minkyu's attention to the younger canine's form.

The dark wolf blushed a little and had to turn away for a moment in order to get any showering done. He turned on the warm water and sighed happily when it hit his body. He let himself get soaked completely before running his paws through his wet fur, enjoying the feeling. The large wolf applied some shampoo to his fur in order to feel completely clean.

The relaxing sound of water hitting the stone tiles they were standing on brought him into a new trance, one he was quickly snapped out of by the white wolf again, as he felt the boy's paws on his back, stroking him gently. Yujin must've felt him startle, because he chuckled lightly and patted his shoulders. "Just helping out a friend by washing his back. Be sure to wash mine too, alright?" he asked before taking the shampoo and applying it to Minkyu's broad back. He seemed to take a certain joy in doing so, judging by the water sent flying in all directions behind him.

The black wolf closed his eyes and sighed happily as the smaller wolf took care of him like that. He'd never done this with any of the other members, so he was quite surprised by Yujin's sudden closeness. Sure, he had fantasized about being with him like that, but he'd never thought that it would actually become a reality at one point. He pinched himself just to make sure he wasn't dreaming. Nope, wide awake. His wagging tail brushed over the slender one's belly, drawing a pleased sound from the boy, which made him wag even faster. This went on for a little while, until the boy turned around.

"My turn now."

Minkyu turned around to the boy and immediately placed his huge paws onto the small white back. It was funny to see how much darker his fur seemed like that, and how much bigger his paws seemed to be. He stroked the boy with surprising gentleness while blushing and smiling. He was really happy that Yujin allowed him to be this close to him. He really liked the wolf, and it wasn't long before his paws moved down onto the slightly curvy hips, softly squeezing them even.

Yujin giggled at that and looked at him over his shoulder. "What are you doing?" he asked softly before lightly swaying his hips from side to side, actually teasing the big wolf.

The group leader bit his lower lip and moved his paws over the boy's chest and stomach, hugging him against his strong body. "I...I don't know..." he said softly in the younger wolf's ear, causing it to flick once. He nuzzled said ear and licked it slowly, causing Yujin to gasp very softly and turn around, which was when Minkyu bent down and slanted his lips over Yujin's, kissing him deeply. He was afraid of the possible reaction, but when the boy melted into the kiss and actually returned it, he held the kiss longer, emboldened by the other one's reaction.

The kiss lasted only a few seconds, but it felt as if entire lifetimes had passed them by, leaving them both panting softly. "I...I'm sorry," Minkyu said softly while blushing brightly and fidgeting with his paws after having let go of him.

"Don't be," Yujin replied while smiling before licking lips. "I have to go now. I'll see you tomorrow, okay?" he asked softly. He nuzzled Minkyu's strong jaw and headed for the door, leaving the black wolf alone with his thoughts.

He turned off the shower and headed for the drying booth, all the while still feeling Yujin's lips on his. He licked them and moved his arms around himself for a moment, imagining the boy in them. The kiss had been amazing, and he was quite certain that Yujin had liked it too. This opened new, very dangerous, doors for him, and he wasn't yet sure if that was a good thing or not. He headed back to his room and went to bed, replaying the kiss over and over in his head until he eventually fell asleep, enjoying dreams filled with visions of the beautiful white wolf and his mesmerizing aquamarine eyes.

"Could you tilt your head a little bit to the side? Yes, perfect! Hold still! Oh, I love that look!"

Minkyu sighed inwardly while giving the camera an annoyed look while posing with a rather beautiful bottle of perfume. Junyoung and he were tasked with shooting pictures for a commercial of a new perfume, the name of which he'd already forgotten. Of all his idol activities, doing photoshoots was the most boring one, according to him. It was just hours of sitting still while people prepped him and kept changing his pose, making sure that the light hit him just right, and that no single strand of fur was out of place. His annoyed look was by no means fake, but it fit the character that he was supposed to portray perfectly, pleasing the photographer.

He dared to steal a look at his friend, who was shooting the second camera lusty and teasing looks, posing accordingly. He was an absolute natural at this, and he enjoyed it to the fullest as well. The brown wolf winked at the cute wolf girl taking care of the lighting. "Hey, beautiful, why don't you come a little closer?" he asked with a husky voice, almost causing the girl to melt into a puddle at the spot, leading the seductive wolf to grin and wag.

"Keep it in your pants, Junyoung. You're not here to pick up girls!" Minkyu said, feeling that it was up to him to keep his friend in check. The last thing they needed right before their debut was some kind of scandal to happen. Not that what the other canine was doing could even be compared to what took place in the showers the previous night. He got warmer under his fur just from thinking about how Yujin's paws had felt on his body, the way they had pressed against each other, and the feeling of that wonderful kiss. He wondered if Yujin was thinking about him too at that moment.

"Uhm...Minkyu? Hello? Excuse me? MINKYU!" the photographer said, trying to get his attention again. The rabbit looked a little annoyed and had obviously been waiting for him to respond.

The black wolf turned his attention back to the man, his ears flat and his tail still for a moment. "Huh? Oh, I'm sorry. Different pose?" he asked before changing his position to one where he was sitting up, legs spread, while leaning on his legs, holding the bottle in one paw, and looking at it. The photographer started shooting pictures again, and he was safe again for a while. That wouldn't be the only time he got distracted during the shoot though.

Several days later, after having returned from participating in a variety show, in which the group had to do all kinds of crazy things and answer weird questions, the group decided to come together in the recording room to practice their new song. It was completely different from the sugar-sweet songs most groups tried to debut with in the annual competition. Minkyu had titled the song "Break Out," with lyrics symbolizing people breaking away from their restrictions and boring lives in order to pursue what they really wanted to do. To the group, it stood for their determination to violently burst forth into the entertainment industry like wildfire. The song was dark and heavy with a lot of bass and cool guitars, as well as awesome sound effects. Yujin and Minkyu were very proud of it, and the rap lyrics that Junyoung came up with fit the theme perfectly, creating a song that the group dared call a masterpiece.

They had practiced the song individually before, and the black wolf had undergone rap training by Junyoung. It turned out that he wasn't as bad at rapping as he'd initially feared, which was a huge boost to his ego, as well as a relief. Minkyu was quite sure that they'd be able to pull off singing the song, as long as they practiced enough and tweaked it a little here and there.

The group gathered around in a circle, each standing in front of a recording mic. They had their lyrics in front of them and waited for their singing coach to start the music. This was one of the few things the group couldn't do themselves, at least not when all of them were singing together. The older rat was a true expert and used to be in an idol group himself many years before them. He held up his thumb to them and started the music after fidgeting with some of the controls.

The group started singing all at once, which went perfectly according to how they had planned it. Minkyu continued with his solo, followed by Seojun, before the song would progress into the chorus, with the twins in the lead, their high voices as beautiful as ever. Yujin was really into the song and couldn't help but look at the black wolf for a moment, causing him to mess up a few words in the lyrics, before he managed to get back into it, earning him a frown from his twin brother. Junyoung's rap part was absolutely flawless, and while Minkyu's was still far from perfect, it wasn't as bad as it could've been. The extra practice sessions with the lead rapper had really helped prepare him for this. The rest of the song was basically singing the chorus a few more times, before it ended.

The group cheered, and most of them were smiling. Seojun was not though. "That wasn't perfect by a long shot. Again, please," he said while looking at the leader.

Minkyu nodded and signaled the coach to start again. The rat wouldn't give his advice until the group specifically asked for it, which was the way they liked it. The song started up again, and it pretty much went okay, except for Minkyu messing up the text in his rap this time. He growled softly in frustration and raked his claw through the fur on his head. "Sorry, guys. This is even harder than I thought it would be," he said.

"You're doing fine. We just need to practice some more," Yujin said while smiling brightly and wagging.

"No, it wasn't fine. He needs to do better. We all have to do better if we want to debut this year," Junyoung said with a seriousness to his voice that was quite unlike him. He seemed determined and frustrated. "Also, Seojun, could you sing a bit lower and more monotonous in your lines? It would sound a lot darker and cooler if you did it like that, I think."

"I'm sorry, hyung, but I don't agree with you. I am not a robot, and I will not sing like one," the gray wolf spoke, crossing his arms and narrowing his eyes just a tad, his hackles rising a bit as well.

Minkyu turned to the rat and smiled apologetically. "I'm sorry, Haneul-hyung, but could you help us out a little? What do you think?" INSTINCT's leader asked the expert, hoping he would shed some light on points to improve on, so the others would stop arguing with each other.

Haneul folded a paw over his chin while he thought deeply about what to say, before pressing the intercom button. "Personally, I think that Junyoung has a point with the monotonous singing. It could sound really cool; however, if Seojun really doesn't want to do it, then he could just sing a little bit lower to give it more of a rough edge," he said calmly. "Also, the twins sound absolutely wonderful together as usual. Great job, boys," he said.

The white wolves wagged happily and fist-bumped before dabbing, causing the rest to chuckle at them. "That dance move is so last month," Seojun said, rolling his eyes.

"Well, we like doing it still, so we don't care," Kiha said before sticking out his tongue and doing the move again for good measure, causing his brother to grin and the gray wolf to roll his eyes again and groaning.

Minkyu smiled at the rat and bowed slightly. "Thank you for your input. Alright, you heard it. Seojun, I'd like you to at least try to sing lower in that part, and I will try to do a better job on the rapping."

The music started again from the beginning, and they sang together again. Seojun sang lower, but with a lot less energy and enthusiasm than before. He clearly wasn't into it. Yujin and

Minkyu were distracted by each other again, causing the white wolf to mess up his lines again, and Minkyu to start on his rap part too late.

Haneul sighed and stopped the music. "Guys, I don't know what's going on, but this sounded worse than just now. Minkyu and Yujin, stick to your lines, they're right in front of you. Seojun, put more energy into it. You sound like you're going to fall asleep," he said sternly while frowning. He'd never seen the group this chaotic before, and it worried him. He made a note of it in his phone before starting the music again. The next try was about as disastrous as the previous one, and the members started accusing each other.

"Seojun, is it really that hard to put a bit more effort into it? You're dragging everyone down!" Junyoung said, his ears back and his hackles raised in frustration.

"You say that, but at least I can remember my lines, or at least read them. I really don't know what's gotten into you two today," the lead choreographer said while looking at the two love birds. It was clear that he was annoyed by them as his eyes shot daggers. He clenched his fists and put away his headphones before walking out of the room, reducing the group to four.

"S...Seojun-hyung!" Yujin called after him, looking worried.

His brother placed a paw on the boy's shoulder and squeezed it. "Oh, I know. Yujin just keeps getting distracted by a certain black wolf. We need your blood in the upper half of your body today, bro. Get your priorities straight," he said sternly with a slight growl. "We don't have time for this."

Yujin turned to his brother with a look of shock and confusion on his face. He couldn't remember the last time Kiha had been that nasty to him. He whined softly and threw off his headphone as well, running out of the room on the verge of crying, leaving only three wolves in the room.

Minkyu could only stare at the group as it fell apart before his eyes. He moved to go after the youngest of the twins, before he was stopped by Junyoung holding his arm. "Leave him. We have more important things to do."

The large wolf bristled and snarled as he pulled himself free and pushed the brown wolf back. "What do you know!? Can't you see that we are in deep shit right now? Practice is over!" he growled before leaving the room as well, leaving two wolves and a rat, who was on the phone in the studio.

"Do you know why I have called you here today, Minkyu?" the old gray wolf opposite INSTINCT's leader asked him as he poured them both a glass of water. This man was the most important man in the agency, the director, meaning he had the power to make or break any potential idol or idol group that was signed with his agency.

The younger black wolf nervously accepted the glass of water and took a sip before putting it back down. There could be various reasons for the man bringing him in, but the most likely reason would be that it was because of what happened during singing practice the previous day. He certainly hoped it wasn't because of what was going on between Yujin and him. As far as he knew, nobody knew exactly what was going on, except maybe Kiha. Damned twins and their supposed spiritual bonds. "Could it be that Haneul-hyung called you, sir? About yesterday?"

The man sipped his water and played with his necktie a little before sighing and turning his wise brown eyes on the idol-to-be. "Minkyu, it is your responsibility to keep your group, your pack so to speak, functioning as a perfect unit. If you cannot do this, then I fear INSTINCT won't be ready to debut anytime soon," he spoke calmly and with worry on his face.

Minkyu bit his lip and his ears went down while he thought on those words. He was responsible. He was the leader, or, as the director would often call him, an Alpha. It was his job to solve the problems in the group, but he had no idea what could possibly work in their case. Everybody just seemed to have a lot of built-up frustration that needed to be let out somehow.

He nodded before lifting his eyes up to the director's. "I understand, sir. I will take care of it."

"See to it that you do. You have about two weeks to get ready for Debut Dome. You can do it, Minkyu. INSTINCT has the potential to win this thing, but you have to find your team spirit back first," he said before nodding at the boy, signaling that the conversation was over.

To relieve some of the stress of problems around him and the heavy burden of trying to solve the current predicament, the large black wolf decided to do what he always did to calm himself down: dance. He would follow it up with a long warm shower, as was his custom, but first he'd distract his worrying mind with music and choreography. He closed the door to the dance room behind him and put down a small bag holding a bottle of water and a towel, before moving over to the music control panel and selecting one of his favorite songs. It wasn't one of their own, but that hardly mattered at the moment. He took his spot in the middle of the room and let his muscle memory take over as he danced his heart out, combining powerful movements with moments of calmer moves. Minkyu let his body do the talking as he freestyled through the song instead of sticking to the choreo.

While moving around in this semi-meditative state, he hadn't heard the door closing, and actually wasn't aware of another presence, until he'd opened his mossy eyes and looked right into the aquamarine blue of Yujin's. They could've been Kiha's as well, of course, but he wouldn't stand as close as this beautiful white wolf was at that moment. Minkyu opened his mouth to say something, only to have the smaller wolf moving a finger over his lips and shaking his head with a smile. The next song came on, which was one of their own, and the younger wolf started dancing as elegantly as the first snow in December, while somehow still dancing the choreography perfectly. The obsidian wolf joined in with a smile, happily moving along according to what he was taught, while his heart was dancing a different dance entirely.

"Mind if we join in?"

The two dancers turned to the door to see the other three members standing there, smiling at them and walking over. Kiha hugged his twin, which started a hugging circle for a moment, at the end of which, everyone was wagging and smiling, ears up all the way.

"Alright, let's just dance our older choreos for a moment, alright? Just for fun," Minkyu said before turning on the music.

The group happily danced together, forgetting all about their worries and frustrations. It seemed everyone just needed a proper distraction to be able to let go of the accumulated stress of standing on the edge of glory. It was time for them to go beyond their limits. There would be time for them to talk about their issues, but not just yet. Not tonight.

The leader looked at his small pack and smiled brightly upon seeing the happy faces and wagging tails. They had found their harmony again, and he felt like nothing could possibly ruin the moment.

"Junyoung, you need more practice. Your dancing was a little sloppy still," the gray wolf said, causing everyone else present to groan and slap their paws over their faces.

Two weeks had passed since that night, and INSTINCT had spent most of their time on reforging their bonds, working out their differences, and getting ready in time for the big show. Time flew by like a cheetah on speed, until the moment they were collected from their apartment and driven over to the capital, where Debut Dome would be held on the biggest and most advanced stage the country had to offer. To say that the boys were nervous about performing in front of over forty thousand people would be the understatement of the year.

The five young wolves were waiting in their dressing room, where a screen was mounted so they could watch the others perform. The only thing the staff needed them to do, was be at the right spot at the right time. After that, the rest of their performance was up to them. Minkyu was going over his rap lyrics again, the twins were playing cards, and Junyoung and

Seojun were going over the choreography again, just marking the positions and moves. The gray and brown wolves had really grown to respect each other more, and they were more likely to listen to each other's feedback now, which was something Minkyu was incredibly grateful for. The group had grown a lot stronger while working toward a common goal.

They were joined by their stylist, as well as two groomers, who would get them ready for their show. The twins went into make-up first, while the others put on their outfits, which consisted of ripped black jeans and open leather jackets, leaving their trained upper bodies exposed. It wasn't very original, but incredibly effective with the mostly-female crowd. The white wolves' fur was brushed to perfection before black eyeliner was added to their look, to make them appear less innocent and pure. The two otter groomers worked very meticulously, making sure every single strand of fur was positioned the way they wanted.

One of the show's staff members came to collect them just seconds after the finishing touches to Minkyu's look were done. He stood up and straightened his vest before fingering the multiple silver earrings in his ears. The leader looked really tough, and it made him grin a little while checking himself out. This was totally going to work out. The group moved to the designated waiting area, where they listened to a sugar-sweet song by some girl group they weren't really familiar with, until it was their time to shine.

They took up their positions on special platforms underneath the stage. They'd practiced on that stage for days, so they knew what to do and what to expect. The music started right after the MC's announced them. Minkyu was shot up from the platform and landed in what could be described as a superhero pose, before getting up and looking menacingly into the crowd as he started singing. The rest was shot up as well as soon as it was their turn to either sing or dance. The crowd was absolutely hyped by the group of handsome wolves dancing together and the performance was absolutely flawless. All of their hard work had definitely paid off. By the time the song had ended, they were all panting and either smiling or grinning. They lined up and bowed deeply.

Minkyu walked over to one of the MCs and took his microphone before addressing the crowd. "We are INSTINCT! Don't even dare cheering for anybody else!" he roared through the mic before taking off his jacket and flexing the muscles he trained so hard for, causing the thousands of people to scream appreciatively. He turned around again and walked off with the others.

They hugged each other in the dressing room and laughed, cheered, and generally celebrated a job well done. It almost didn't matter if they'd win anymore. Almost. They were simply really pleased and happy that everything had gone this well. Minkyu cleared his throat and requested the others' attention for a moment. "I just want to say how incredibly proud I am of what we have achieved as a group. What we did out there just now was definitely our best performance ever, and we couldn't have done it without each other. I couldn't have done it without you, so…thank you all," he said and smiled brightly.

"Urgh, you're so sappy. We love you for it though," Junyoung said as he playfully punched his leader on the shoulder. The rest laughed and agreed.

The groomers touched them up for the reward ceremony, which they were looking forward to by then. Anxiety struck as soon as all groups were called up onto the stage though. INSTINCT joined all of the other groups, being welcomed by thousands of cheers that hit them like a tidal wave. They suddenly weren't that sure of themselves anymore, and could only hope that the audience wouldn't see it. They had done all they could've done to make this performance a success. Now they just needed a little luck.

The MCs, a beautiful lioness and a handsome stallion moved to the middle of the stage. "The time has come to announce the winners of tonight's contest!" the lioness spoke, her voice washing over the crowd and causing them to grow silent.

"We will begin by stating that each and every group here tonight has done remarkably well. They have worked hard to stand here! Give them a big hand, ladies and gentlemen!" the horse said while raising his fist into the air, firing up the crowd into producing a booming applause, which did absolutely nothing to ease the knots of excitement in the five wolves' stomachs.

"That may be so, but there can only be one true winner. We will begin by announcing third place," the lioness said, holding up a card. The entire stadium grew silent, which was quite an amazing feat, since it was packed with over ten thousand people of different species. "Third place is taken by...VERTIGOOOOO!" the lioness roared. Said idol group took a step forward and bowed deeply before taking a step back again, their faces not entirely happy, but not too disappointed either.

A relieved sigh went through the remaining idol groups, who were all hoping to win the grand prize. Their relief was short-lived, as the horse started talking. "Congratulations, VERTIGO. Next up, our second place...Ladies and gentlemen, give it up for CELESTIIIIITE!"

INSTINCT was getting more nervous with each passing second, and Minkyu was quite sure he'd lose it, until he felt his right paw being taken, fingers lacing through his. He looked down to see Yujin smiling up at him, giving his big paw a gentle squeeze. The black wolf smiled back and turned to his left before taking Junyoung's paw, who in turn took Seojun's. They smiled at each other, and the leader turned to look at Yujin again, who had taken his brother's paw as well. United they stood, ready to take on the world. There was only one spot left. The ultimate prize they had worked so hard for was within reach. It was being dangled in front of them like a catnip toy in front of a feral cat.

"Now, the moment we have all been waiting for, the idol groups behind me possibly even more so than any of you lovely people out there, is finally here! The winners...of tonight's show... the group who has received the highest score...the group who will be promised their debut… Can you feel the tension in the air, people?" the lioness asked while grinning.

Some of the idol groups groaned softly, hating the fact that they were being teased at that very moment. The five friends had their heads down, and if they squeezed each other's paws even harder, something would definitely break. They were holding their breaths, waiting for the final verdict.

"Stop teasing them, Jess. It is time to give everybody the answer they so desperately crave! The moment of truth, ladies and gentlemen! The ultimate winner of Debut Dome is…"

INSTINCT. INSTINCT. Please, let it be INSTINCT! Minkyu thought strongly while grinding his teeth together and trembling.

The horse held the card in his paw and grinned before throwing it up into the air. "INSTIIIIINCT!"

Fire shot up from the stage, the wonderful pyrotechnics illustrating perfectly how the group was feeling at that very moment. They started yelling and hugging each other before being called up to the middle of the stage. Minkyu was handed a microphone and the trophy, and was asked to say a few words.

The leader handed the trophy to Seojun before speaking. "I would like to thank all of you for being here and for putting your faith in us. Winning this contest means a great deal to us, but there is still one thing left here tonight that I want," he said before handing the mic back to the MC. He pulled Yujin up to him and looked down at him with a smile. His next words were only for those standing close enough to hear it.

"Yujin, I love you," he said, cupping the beautiful boy's cheek in his paw, before kissing him deeply right there on stage, in front of the whole world.

ABOUT THE ARTIST
Daniie

Daniies_Doodles has been drawing since she was a wee child. Always drawing everything she saw in front of her and in her mind. Daniie enjoys reading, and nature. Daniie is in college to continue her pursuit and love of art.